UNHOLY GROUND

When midwife Maudie Rouse marries the love of her life, policeman Dick Bryant, the pair could not be happier as they settle into contented domesticity in the village of Llandyfan. But troubles abound for the newlyweds — an abandoned baby, a difficult new district nurse, and the possibility of losing their home — and Maudie must find a way to deal with the problems, in addition to bicycling around the village performing her professional duties. Meanwhile, a grim discovery is made in a local farmer's field . . .

Books by Catriona McCuaig
in the Linford Mystery Library:

THE MIDWIFE AND THE MURDER
BLOOD LINES
BLOOD MONEY
FACE FROM THE PAST

CATRIONA McCUAIG

UNHOLY
GROUND

A Midwife Maudie mystery

Complete and Unabridged

LINFORD
Leicester

First published in Great Britain

First Linford Edition
published 2016

A catalogue record for this book is available
from the British Library.

ISBN 978–1–4448–2845–0

Published by
F. A. Thorpe (Publishing)
Anstey, Leicestershire

Set by Words & Graphics Ltd.
Anstey, Leicestershire
Printed and bound in Great Britain by
T. J. International Ltd., Padstow, Cornwall

This book is printed on acid-free paper

1

Midwife Maudie Rouse looked at the radiant woman in the mirror and smiled shyly. 'I think I'm glad you talked me into buying this hat,' she murmured, turning to her friend, 'but tell me the truth, now; you are sure it's not too girlish, aren't you? I don't want to go swanning down the aisle like mutton dressed as lamb.'

'Nonsense, of course you won't!' The vicar's wife smiled gently at her friend. 'Besides, if a bride can't look pretty on her wedding day, it's a poor lookout for womanhood! And that new hairstyle has taken years off you, my dear. It almost tempts me to get my own grey locks lopped off!'

Maudie had to admit that the new short hairstyle suited her well, and it was certainly easier to keep tidy than the bun she'd worn for so long. A quick flip through her curls with a damp comb in the morning, and she was ready for action. Today, though, she'd invested in a professional shampoo and set, and the hairdresser had shown her how to position the cheeky little hat to its best advantage. It was a delicious little straw confection, almost brimless, trimmed with matching artificial daisies and a tiny veil that skimmed her eyebrows.

She looked down at her dress with satisfaction. Made from rose-pink silk, it had a plain, round neckline, and full sleeves that ended in fitted cuffs above the elbow. 'This dress makes me feel like a queen,' she said, smoothing the material over her hips. 'It was a terrible extravagance, though. I'm afraid to tell Dick what I paid for it. All that money for something I'll only wear once.'

'That is quite enough of that!' Joan Blunt responded in mock severity. 'And it will certainly come in handy now and again if you wear it with a jacket, or maybe a sleeveless coat; navy linen, perhaps, with a navy hat to go with it.' She giggled. 'And you're not the only one who can keep a secret! If Harold ever finds out what I paid for this costume he'll have a fit! He'll think I robbed the poor-box!' She patted her blue linen coat and skirt lovingly. She wore it with a white silk blouse, tied with a floppy bow at the neck, which had been a gift to the matron of honour from Maudie and Dick.

The clock struck the quarter hour. 'Well, this is it, Nurse! Are you ready to take the plunge? It's time we were getting over to the church.'

Maudie gulped. 'Yes, it's now or never! And if Dick Bryant doesn't show up, I'll kill him; I will, really!'

'Of course he'll come! He's probably standing at the altar this very minute, quaking in his policeman's boots. And I know you can't possibly be having second thoughts,' Mrs Blunt said firmly, 'so off we go, quick march!'

Maudie had indeed experienced a few qualms, although they had nothing to do with marrying Dick as such. But when you were about to wed for the first time at the age of forty, it was only natural to wonder if you might be too set in your ways to adjust happily to sharing a home with another person. And at forty-five, it was the first time around for Dick, too. How was he feeling at this very moment? *Oh, well, too late for second thoughts now*, she told herself.

Joan Blunt had dressed the bride in the vicarage rather than in Maudie's cottage, on the theory that it was closer to the church, so they could walk there with less fear of being blown about if the weather worsened. A few onlookers had already gathered at the wrought-iron gates to see the bride, and Maudie was heartened by the encouraging words called to her by the local women.

Three small boys followed her halfway up the path, singing: 'Here comes the bride, all dressed in pink . . . '

Maudie couldn't imagine what was coming next, and she didn't want to find out. There were not many words that rhymed with pink; in fact, she could think of one or two epithets that no bride wished to hear on her wedding day.

'Grr!' She took a threatening step towards the boys and they dodged away, laughing. She had ushered all three of the little rascals into the world, and they knew each other well.

The swelling sound of organ music reached them as one of the churchwardens opened the door to admit the bride and her attendant. 'Good luck, Nurse!' he whispered. Oliver Bassett was a local farmer whose grandchildren Maudie had delivered. It seemed only fitting that the people she knew in her everyday life should be on hand now to wish her well.

As she made her way down the aisle to join her bridegroom, she noted with surprise that the church was filled with flowers, all of them in shades of pink and white. Cosmos, pinks, sweet peas and more. There were far too many to have come from a single garden. By the looks of it, someone had organized this, and it seemed that half the village must have contributed to the display. This realization brought tears to her eyes, and she blinked them away before they could make her mascara run. Accustomed as she was to being out in all winds and weathers, she seldom wore makeup other than a dab of powder and a smear of lipstick. She had practised carefully for her day of days, and she didn't want to arrive at the altar steps looking like a raccoon.

Dick Bryant, looking unusually spruce in his new grey suit, turned towards her with a smile as she arrived at his side. Someone had provided him with a small pink rosebud for his lapel that exactly matched the pink of her bridal frock. She suspected Joan Blunt's hand in all this floral glory. She must remember to thank her later.

She smothered a grin at the sight of the best man, standing rigidly to attention at Dick's side. Constable Bill Brewer was an all-round good chap, to quote Dick, but he did have trouble with his hair. Maudie had threatened Dick with awful warnings about what she was likely to say if poor Bill showed up at their wedding with his hair looking like a startled lavatory brush. Bill had taken the hint — and had it all shaved down, so that now he looked like an American mobster fresh out of jail. Oh, well, she supposed his heart was in the right place, poor lad. Give him full marks for trying.

In no time at all, it seemed, Maudie and Dick had exchanged their vows and he had planted the obligatory kiss on her cheek. She glanced down at her left hand, where a plain gold ring winked up at her in the sunlight. It had happened! They had done it! She was Mrs Dick Bryant!

★　★　★

The reception was held in the parish hall. Neither Maudie nor Dick had any close relations living, so they had decided not to have a proper wedding breakfast. Or was 'breakfast' the right name for such a feast, held in the middle of the afternoon? One way or another, Maudie knew everyone for miles around, and to have invited some people and not the rest would have given terrible offence. In rural places such slights have been known to start feuds lasting for centuries!

Instead they had opted for a stand-up reception, with tea and sandwiches provided by the Women's Institute in co-operation with the Mothers' Union; with, of course, the wedding cake to follow. That way people could pop in, congratulate the newlyweds, drink a cup of tea, and stay or leave as it suited them.

Tears welled up in Maudie's eyes again during the speeches, when Oliver Bassett got up to say a few kind words about her. 'Nurse has brought so much happiness into our community with the births of our children, never mind the loving care she has given us all in time of trouble. It's her turn now, and I'm sure we all wish her every happiness for the future with her new husband.'

'And may all your troubles be little ones!' someone bawled, earning a reproachful glance from the vicar.

'And on behalf of the parish council, I am delighted to present Mr and Mrs Bryant with this purse,' Bassett concluded, handing Dick an envelope to prolonged applause.

'Where's the purse, Mummy?' a little voice piped up. 'He said he's giving them a purse and I want to see it.'

'Hush, dear. It's just an expression. It means they are being given some money.'

'Why?'

'Well, so they can buy themselves a present, I suppose. They can spend it on something they really want. For their new home, perhaps.'

'And where will that new home be, Nurse?' another voice broke in. 'You'll have to give up your cottage now, won't you, what with it being tied to the job? And of course you'll be giving up nursing too, now you're a married woman.'

Maudie swung round to reply to the little woman at her elbow.

'Actually, it's no on both counts, Mrs Foster. There's a new young nurse arriving soon but she doesn't want the cottage. Her parents aren't keen on her living alone, so she'll be staying with her auntie over in the prefabs. And while she'll be doing the general nursing around the district, I'll still be handling the midwifery, at least for now.'

'Ah, well, I suppose that's a good thing. You'd have time on your hands otherwise. It's not as if you'll be starting a family, is it? Not at your age. But what about your poor hubby, then? A nasty old journey to work on a winter morning, that will be!'

Typical of the rural mind, Maudie thought. The police station at Midvale was only twelve miles away. She made it sound like the far side of the moon.

'Oh, don't you worry about me,' Dick chimed in cheerfully. 'My days at Midvale are numbered. I've got a promotion and I'm on the detective side now. Detective Sergeant Dick Bryant, that's me!'

'Fancy!'

'The powers that be are giving me a car, and they're quite happy to have a presence here at Llandyfan, after all the little problems you've had here recently.'

Llandyfan was an idyllic village, on the English side of the border with Wales, and there had indeed been a series of murders locally in the past few years. In fact, that was how Maudie had first met Dick, when she had come across a body while taking a short cut through a wood near Oliver Bassett's farm.

Since then, Maudie had become embroiled in several other nasty mysteries, culminating in the affair of a fraudulent doctor who had threatened her life. In fact, for a while it had been touch and go whether she would survive to attend her wedding at all.

All those adventures were safely behind her now. In future, Dick had informed her, he would be the one doing all the detecting, and she would be safe at home. And she agreed that she would be glad of that. Or would she?

2

'Where are you going on your honey-moon, Nurse?' One of Maudie's young mothers looked at her, wide-eyed.

'That's a state secret!' Dick told the girl, raising his eyebrows at her and making her giggle.

'Speaking of which, my dear,' he remarked, turning to his new wife, 'if we're to catch that six o'clock train, isn't it time you went home to change? If you don't get moving we'll be forced to spend our honeymoon in Llandyfan, and that would never do!'

Now it was Maudie's turn to giggle. Although it was known only to a few close friends, they did indeed intend to do just that, after laying a few red herrings in the best tradition of the village mystery.

This being the third week of July, all the seaside boarding houses would be crammed with families and shrieking children, hardly places to visit for a peaceful retreat. A posh hotel was out of the question because Maudie hated the thought of breakfasting in a formal hotel dining room, with other guests observing them and speculating on their newlywed status. And why spend their precious holiday time on crowded buses and trains if they could have all the comforts of home?

Their plan was to go to the station, ostensibly to board a train destined for a place unknown. Dick's police colleagues had promised to create a diversion, aided and abetted by Mrs Blunt. The Bryants would sneak back to Maudie's cottage — Maudie and *Dick's* cottage now, of course — batten down the hatches, and enjoy a carefree few days cut off from the world. Some people might find that odd; but, as Maudie well knew, her home could be like Paddington Station at times. Beside the usual distress calls from patients' husbands, there was always a steady flow of people collecting for charity, neighbours wanting to borrow a cup of sugar, and passing ramblers asking for directions.

Maudie scrambled into her going-away costume, which consisted of a beige linen suit and tan pumps with a matching handbag, and in due course was joined by Dick, suitably attired in a tweed jacket and flannel bags. Squashed in the back of Bill Brewer's battered Austin Seven, they were waved away by a cheering crowd, and their great adventure had begun.

'Now, let me get this straight,' Dick said. 'We go into the station yard and straight through the waiting room to the other side.'

'And pray there's nobody on the platform who knows us,' Maudie added.

'There won't be, they're all back at the parish hall. Then we nip over the stile and make our way down Cherry Lane.'

'Not until you hear the sirens,' Bill cut in. 'The lads are going to drive through the village with all the sirens blaring like mad, so everyone will think something is up. While they're all trying to find out what's going on, you two can slip in through Maudie's back door, and Bob's your uncle!'

'The tricky part is going to be getting

past the shop without Ma Hatch seeing us,' Maudie moaned. 'It's all open country there; nowhere to hide. That's where Mrs Blunt comes in. She's going to keep Mrs Hatch busy out at the back somehow. Let's hope it works!'

'I wish you two could hear yourselves,' Bill told them, shaking his head. 'This does happen to be 1950, you know! The war is over! Anybody would think you were a couple of spies, going into enemy territory! What does it matter if people know you're at home? If anyone comes knocking, just don't answer the door!'

'It's easy to see you're not a country boy, Bill Brewer!' Maudie said. 'If I didn't come to the door somebody might think there had been an accident, or I'd been taken ill. If they didn't actually break the door down, they'd at least put in a call to you lot.'

'Funny sort of accident, with both of you out of commission,' Bill muttered. 'Unless there was a gas leak, of course.'

'No, no, we don't have gas.'

'There you are, then. Well, here's the

15

station. Off you go, and don't forget your suitcases!'

* * *

'I wish we *had* forgotten these bally cases!' Dick groaned, as he marched along, weighed down by two bulging cardboard cases. 'What on earth did you put in yours? It weighs a ton!'

'Never mind that!' Maudie muttered. 'If you had to stagger along on these high heels, you'd have something to complain about! Whose silly idea was this, anyway?'

'I seem to recall it was yours, old girl. Listen! There go the sirens now. Everything's going according to plan. Better get down: we're coming to the cottages now.'

Bent double, and giggling like children playing cops and robbers, they shuffled past a low hedge separating cottage gardens from the lane. The voices of children at play floated to them from behind the privet, and at one point they thought they were about to be discovered when a small terrier rushed at them, yapping madly. Maudie smacked it on the

16

snout with her white glove and it retreated with its tail between its legs, leaving her feeling guilty.

When at last they reached the cottage and rushed inside, bolting the back door behind them, she fell into a chair, gasping. 'Ouch, I'm sure I've got blisters! Remind me never to run over rough ground in high heels again!' She kicked off her shoes and bent over to rub her foot.

'I'd rather remind you that we became man and wife this afternoon,' Dick said, pulling her to her feet and into his arms.

'After what we just did, I think I've married a crazy man!' she told him, laughing.

'Speak for yourself! But yes, I must indeed be out of my mind to have gone along with a stunt like this. I don't see why we couldn't have put a notice on the front door saying 'Do Not Disturb', just as we might have done in a hotel bedroom.'

'But it was fun, though, wasn't it?' A sense of deep satisfaction crept over Maudie at that moment. If they could laugh at the same events and do silly things together without feeling self-conscious, then surely their marriage had a good chance of succeeding. And then, when she felt Dick's lips on hers, she knew without a doubt that he was the one and only man for her, and that she had been right to stand before the altar in St John's church that day and pledge her love to him for as long as they both should live. Whatever trials and tribulations the future might bring, they would weather them together, and she knew that any problems would surely be interlaced with all the joys that life might hold.

3

On Thursday morning, Maudie opened all the curtains to let the sunshine in. The idea was to let people think that the couple had returned on the late train on Wednesday, if they thought about it at all.

'Thank goodness for that!' Dick said, as he forked over a rasher of bacon that was sizzling in the pan. 'It was like being back in the wartime blackout days in here.'

That, of course, was an exaggeration, because even with the substantial lining the chintz curtains let in plenty of daylight. Maudie didn't bother to respond. They still had three days' holiday remaining before they had to return to their respective jobs, and Dick intended to spend it pottering in the garden, or taking his wife on long rambles around the countryside. After years of pedalling about visiting her patients, Maudie was already very familiar with the terrain; but, as Dick pointed out, you saw different things when you went on foot.

She had hardly doused the breakfast dishes in a sink full of soapy water when their first visitor arrived. It was the vicar's wife, bearing a small pot of honey and a cardboard box.

'I noticed you were back,' she said, giggling because she knew they hadn't been away. 'I brought you this honey as a welcome-home gift, and this is the top layer of the wedding cake. I managed to whisk it away from the hall before the Scouts could get their greedy little hands on it.'

'Oh, good!' Dick said. 'I'll have a piece of that now! I didn't get any at the reception!'

'You'll do no such thing, Mr Bryant! This must be put away and kept for — er — some special occasion!'

Maudie understood why her friend's cheeks had turned pink. Of course, it was traditional that one layer of the wedding cake was kept back for use at the christening of a couple's first child, which in the old days had often occurred within the first year of marriage. Sadly, there would be no such happy event for Maudie and Dick.

'Perhaps we'll have an anniversary party this time next year,' she suggested.

'There won't be an anniversary if I die of starvation in the meantime,' Dick grumbled.

'And that won't happen any time soon,' Maudie reminded him, having just watched him pack away three rashers of bacon, two eggs and a fried tomato.

★   ★   ★

Monday morning came all too soon. Dick drove off to Midvale to meet his new boss, a certain Detective Inspector Bob Goodwood. 'Have a nice day, love,' he instructed Maudie, planting a husbandly kiss on her cheek. 'What do you intend doing while I'm gone?'

'Need you ask? This is Monday!' Every housewife in Llandyfan did her laundry on Monday, with the exception of young mothers who had to get their infants' nappies out several times a week. Getting your washing on the line before ten in the morning was vital if you didn't want to be branded as a lazy good-for-nothing, and the non-coloured items had to be sparkling white if you wanted to escape criticism from your female neighbours.

Humming cheerfully, Maudie divided the items into piles according to the treatment they required, frowning at one of Dick's new socks that was already sporting a hole in the toe. She had just put their face flannels in a pot on the range to boil when the doorbell rang. Muttering to herself, she flung the door open.

The girl on the doorstep looked as if a good puff of wind might blow her over. Thin as a stray cat, and pale with it, if you could see past all the freckles on her sad little face. Her spiky ginger hair was cropped around her ears, and her eyes were such a faded blue as to be almost silver. She had evidently arrived by bicycle because a battered machine was propped up against the gatepost.

'Can I help you?' Maudie asked, wiping her hands on her apron.

'Um, I'm Melanie. Melanie Gregg.'

'Oh, yes?'

'I'm the new nurse.'

'Oh, I see. You'd better come in, then. They told me somebody new had been taken on, but I didn't catch the name. Do you mind coming through to the kitchen? I'm afraid I'm rather busy at the moment.'

If she was truly a qualified nurse, this girl must be considerably older than she looked, which was about fourteen! And possibly she wasn't always this timid; it was only natural that she should be a bit nervous about starting a new job, and meeting her opposite number for the first time. Maudie could well recall her training days, and how it felt to be reporting to some fearsome nursing sister when assigned to a new ward.

She smiled, indicating Dick's chair at the kitchen table. 'Now then, Nurse Gregg! Tell me all about yourself. Staying with your auntie, aren't you?'

'That's right, Nurse Bryant. That's why I took this job, you see, so I could go to Auntie June. Dad didn't like the idea of me living alone, and he knew she'd look after me. She's his older sister, you know.'

'That's nice.'

'But when Dad hears what sort of place this is I've come to, he'll want to me to go back home, quick sharp!'

'Oh, really? Why would that be, then?' Maudie frowned, although she could guess what was coming next.

'All those murders, of course! And as for that surgery! It's not safe to go there, is it? Auntie says the big house must be cursed, that's what!'

'I suppose we have had a bit of bad luck,' Maudie murmured, knowing as she said it that her explanation was thin, to say the least. Cora Beasley, the lady of the manor, had converted the gatehouse on her estate into a surgery for the use of her nephew, Dr Len Lennox. All had gone well until his cousin had killed a young woman who had spurned his attentions, leaving the doctor to take the blame.

'That really had nothing to do with the doctor, or his surgery,' Maudie explained now, suppressing a shudder as she remembered how closely she and Mrs

Beasley had come to falling victim to the murderous Bingo Munro. 'Those people were outsiders, and the trouble happened long before they arrived in Llandyfan.'

Melanie was not convinced. 'Auntie says you've had other murders, and you were mixed up in them.'

'It's a wicked world, Nurse. Murders happen everywhere, unfortunately.'

'Somebody should have told me about that fake doctor they've just got rid of. How on earth did he get taken on here in the first place? Auntie says they mustn't have taken proper care looking into his professional credentials if a thing like that could happen.'

It seemed to Maudie that Auntie had a great deal too much to say for herself! 'I'm surprised your aunt didn't mention it,' she said. 'About Dr Ransome, I mean. That is, the man we all believed to be Dr Ransome.'

The girl shrugged. 'I'm getting a living allowance, and Auntie needs the money. She's only got her widow's pension and it doesn't stretch very far, not these days. And I've signed a contract with the council now, so I'm stuck here for a year at least. Mind you, if we get any more murders, I'm off, and they can stick their contract!

'There won't be any more murders,' Maudie assured her. 'We've had enough violence hereabouts to last us for a lifetime. And my husband is a police detective,' she added proudly, 'and with him in the village, any potential criminal will be frightened off. Now then, Nurse, I think that's enough silly talk for one day! Let's discuss your job. I thought I might come with you on your rounds at first to introduce you to your patients. What do you say?'

The girl tossed her shaggy head. 'I'm quite capable of dealing with people on my own, Nurse! Nothing was said about you being my superior! I was told I'd be taking over the general nursing cases in the district, leaving you free to look after the midder patients.'

Maudie silently counted to ten. 'I was simply making a friendly gesture, Nurse Gregg, but if you prefer to start out on your own, that is your privilege. Some of the farms in the outlying areas are hard to find and I thought I could save you from getting lost. It could be important if you're called out to an emergency.'

The girl's mouth set in a stubborn line. 'Auntie June can give me directions if necessary, thank you very much!'

When the young nurse left on her bicycle Maudie watched her go, shaking her head sadly. 'That child has more prickles than a hedgehog,' she muttered as she closed the door and returned to her chores. She had no wish to bully the girl, but it would have been useful for her to know her patients' idiosyncrasies, and the peculiarities of their situations. John Grover's bulldog, for instance, always made a great show of snapping and snarling, but he wouldn't hurt a fly. Old Mrs Castor always offered tea, but it was wise to refuse because she mixed it with bitter-tasting herbs of her own gathering, and an attack of the collywobbles was likely to be the result!

Then, too, there might be times when two heads were better then one. Melanie Gregg might be glad of Maudie's help when she had a heavy stroke patient to turn in his bed, and indeed there might be times when Maudie herself would be thankful for an extra pair of hands in a difficult confinement if no doctor was available.

Maudie took a nailbrush to Dick's shirt collar, scrubbing furiously, telling herself to take a few deep breaths and calm down. Why waste time fuming over the silly little chit? The girl had to learn, and learn she would before she was very much older! Let her find out for herself the pitfalls that awaited her in Llandyfan, where the inhabitants always regarded newcomers with suspicion.

In a way, it was too bad they'd got off on the wrong foot. Maudie had looked forward to exchanging confidences over cups of tea with a fellow nurse, recounting past experiences, but obviously that wasn't about to happen. Drat the girl for being so prickly! Never mind, that wasn't as much of a disappointment as it might once have been. She had Dick to talk to now!

4

The telephone rang suddenly, startling Maudie. Her hand shook and the tea she was pouring missed Dick's cup and splashed onto the tablecloth. Muttering, she dabbed at it with a napkin. It had been a wedding present and she didn't want it to stain.

She let Dick deal with the intrusion; after three weeks of marriage he had come to accept the cottage and everything in it as his own home, and he didn't think twice about answering the phone when it rang.

Drat! The tablecloth was already becoming discoloured. Hastily moving the remains of breakfast to the sideboard, she whipped off the cloth and hurried with it to the kitchen. As she rinsed it under the tap she could hear Dick's side of the conversation: the call seemed to be for him.

'The vicarage? Pram left empty? Yes,

yes. I'll run over there at once. It's just up the street.' He rang off. 'Maudie? I have to go out. I don't know how long I'll be. See you later, all right?'

Maudie re-entered the room to find him struggling to put on his jacket. 'Who was that? What's going on?'

'Nothing for you to worry about, my love. I'll tell you all about it later, if there's anything you should know.'

'Don't give me that, Dick Bryant! What was that I heard you say about the vicarage and an empty pram?'

Dick gave her a hasty kiss. 'None of your business, love! What have I said about you staying out of police cases from now on? I'm not having you running into danger again now I'm here to protect you!'

'Babies *are* my business, or have you forgotten?'

'Not this time, old girl!' Dick rushed out of the door, letting it swing to behind him.

'We'll see about that!' Maudie said under her breath. Snatching up a cardigan, for the morning was cool despite the fact they were still in August, she left by the back door, meaning to take the back lane to the graveyard and from there to the vicarage. Once she was on the scene Dick could hardly make her go away, especially if there was a distraught woman to console.

By the sound of things, a baby had been stolen from its pram; without a doubt it must be a child that she had brought into the world herself, and not too long ago. But when she arrived at the front door of the vicarage, she was surprised to find not an empty pram but one that most definitely held a squalling infant. Instinctively, she took hold of the handle and began to jiggle the pram back and forth. The roars of outrage slowed to a plaintive mewling.

A murmur of voices alerted Maudie to the arrival of people coming out of the vicarage. A woman holding a baby to her chest; the vicar, wringing his hands; and Dick, frowning when he caught sight of his wife.

'And like I said,' the young mother was saying, 'I came here to talk to the vicar about Darren's christening, and I didn't want to leave the baby outside with all these flies about, so I took him in with me. When we came back out to go home, I found this other baby in Darren's pram! I've no idea who he is, or what he's doing there! I say he, but it could be a girl for all I know, dressed in green rompers like that!'

'Absolutely shocking!' the vicar mumbled. 'Such wickedness to abandon a helpless infant. I suppose it's the offspring of some unwed mother, although I can't think of any such woman in my parish at the moment. I suppose this is your province, Nurse,' he continued, catching sight of Maudie.

'Well, she needn't think I'm going to look after her beastly baby, whoever she is,' the pram's owner snapped. 'I have enough to do, looking after this one. My hubby would have a fit if he came home from work and found me with two babies in the house. You'd better take him home with you, Nurse.'

'I suppose you'd better do just that,' Dick agreed, acknowledging Maudie for

32

the first time. 'I'll have to put some feelers out to trace this little cuckoo's people.'

'Oh, there's no need for that,' she told him, tilting her chin. 'I know exactly who this is. It's young Peggy Ann Ramsey.'

'What! Are you sure?'

'Of course I'm sure! Didn't I bring her into the world myself just a few weeks ago?' Maudie stooped down to pick up the baby girl, cooing to her lovingly. 'You may as well take Darren home, Mrs Dawson. We can manage here.' She hesitated. 'That's if you don't need Mrs Dawson any longer, Dick?'

He shook his head. 'No, no. It all seems pretty straightforward to me. I'll just hear what the vicar has to say, and then we'll be on our way as well.'

At that moment Joan Blunt came round the corner, pausing for a moment to greet Ella Dawson, who told her story once again with a great deal of nodding and twitching,

Still showing signs of distress, the vicar allowed his wife to shepherd the little group indoors, where she immediately put the kettle on for tea.

'So this is the baby who was abandoned, is it?' She tickled little Peggy Ann under the chin. 'What a pretty dear! Who wouldn't want a lovely lickle baby like you, den?'

'That is what we need to find out,' Dick said, turning to the vicar. 'Can you shed any light on this, Mr Blunt?'

'All I can tell you is that young Mrs Dawson came to see me to set a date for her little boy's christening. I must confess that our meeting took longer than it might have done because I tried to prevail upon her to choose a different baptismal name for the child. She wants to call him Darren. What's wrong with the tried and true Bible names? I asked her. John, say, or Philip . . . '

'Really, Harold, we have to move with the times,' his wife interrupted. 'People simply don't give their children names like Obadiah or Malachi any more, and I understand that Darren is quite popular in America. I was reading about a singer called Darren somebody in a magazine at the hairdresser's'

'David and Matthew are still perfectly

acceptable, Joan! And what about Jonathan or Mark?'

'And then what happened?' Dick prompted.

The vicar screwed up his face in painful thought. 'Why, nothing. The young woman insisted that Darren was the name she wanted, I gave her a date for the baptism, and she went away. A moment later there was a scream from the garden and I dashed out, thinking she'd fallen and hurt herself. She was standing there pointing at the pram, and when I got closer I saw a baby lying on top of the blanket. The baby that Nurse is holding now,' he added. 'Well, it was obvious that somebody had abandoned the child, so I came back in and called the authorities at Midvale.'

'You might have called Nurse,' his wife remarked. 'She's practically next door. And, come to that, Detective Sergeant Bryant was right on the spot. Why phone Midvale?'

'I was too shocked to think straight, dear. It's not every day we find an abandoned baby here, like Moses in the bulrushes! Anyway, what does it matter? Nurse is in charge of the child now, so all's well that ends well.'

Dick asked a few more questions, but it was obvious that the vicar had nothing more to contribute, so, declining offers of tea, the Bryants left for home.

'I suppose I'd better drive over and see what the Ramsey woman has to say for herself,' Dick said when they entered their cottage. 'You'd better keep the baby here until we've decided what to do with it.'

'What do you mean? We'll return her to poor Sheila, of course.'

Dick frowned. 'I'm grateful to you for identifying the baby so quickly, Maudie. That has saved me a lot of legwork, I know. But in this case you must allow me to decide what is best. I'll go and speak to the mother — to her husband too, if I can get hold of him — and try to determine the circumstances that led to the woman's behaviour.'

'And then what will happen?'

'I shall call in social services, and probably this poor little scrap will go to a foster home, at least until the case comes up before the magistrates.'

'Dick! No! Surely it doesn't have to go that far!'

'Child abandonment is a crime, old girl. I can't just turn a blind eye to it. Anything could have happened to this baby if little Mrs Dawson hadn't come on the scene when she did.'

Maudie sank down on a chair, cradling the baby on her knee. 'I want to come with you, Dick. And never mind pulling a face like that at me! Yes, I know what you're going to say: this is police business. Well, I won't deny that, but it's also my business. Sheila Ramsey is one of my patients and I know the background to this case, if that's what you want to call it. It's my belief she's suffering from post-natal depression, and that may have prompted her to do something she's probably regretting by now.'

'I'm not sure I understand what that is,' Dick said.

'My point exactly! So, do I come with you, or do I not?'

★ ★ ★

When the unmarked car drew up in front of the Ramseys' neat semi, Maudie nipped out smartly, clutching the baby, and dashed to the back door of the house. Sheila Ramsey was in enough trouble without nosey neighbours getting in on the act.

The door flew open to reveal a tear-stained woman who reached out to the baby with a glad cry. Ignoring the outstretched arms, Maudie slipped past her into the kitchen, her glance taking in the piles of dirty crockery and the table that still bore the dried-up remains of earlier meals.

'This is my husband, Detective Sergeant Dick Bryant,' she said when Dick had followed them in, closing the door firmly behind him. 'He'd like to have a word with you, Sheila. Peggy Ann wants changing. I'll just see to that and then I'll put her down. No need to come with me. I can find my way.'

When Maudie returned to the kitchen she found Sheila Ramsey sitting at the table in sullen silence, while Dick looked on helplessly. 'I wanted to make Mrs Ramsey a cuppa,' he explained, 'but I can't seem to find a clean . . . ' His voice trailed off.

Mrs Ramsey sighed. 'I'm a bit behind this morning. I haven't got around to doing the washing-up yet.'

Nor for a good many mornings by the look of it, Maudie surmised, rolling up her sleeves to tackle the mess. 'You'll feel better after a strong cup of tea,' she told the wilting woman. 'I'll have one ready in a jiffy, and then you can tell us what all this silly nonsense is about! I know you love that little girl of yours, so what on earth were you doing leaving her all alone in the vicarage garden?'

'She just won't stop crying, Nurse! Morning, noon and night she screams her head off, and I just don't know how to stop it! If only I could get some sleep it wouldn't be as bad, but I'm lucky if I can manage half an hour between bouts of howling. I put her down, I crawl back into bed, and then just as I start to nod off she's off again. My hubby complains about it all the time. I've got the neighbours banging on the wall, and I just don't get a minute to myself to try to relax.'

'So you decided to take her to the vicarage?' Dick asked. 'I've heard of babies being left on church steps, but those are usually newborns with single mothers.'

Maudie shot him a fierce look and he frowned at her in return. Mrs Ramsey appeared not to notice.

'The only way I can get her to stop crying is to walk her in the pram,' she explained. 'The movement seems to soothe her, you see. So I went down the lane with her, and when I came to the church I thought I'd go and sit on one of the benches in the graveyard. It's so peaceful there. I picked her up but she started to grizzle, so I started walking round with her until she calmed down. Then I laid her down in the pram, only I suppose it was the wrong one. When I got home and I didn't have her with me, I couldn't think where she'd gone.'

Dick could keep silent no longer. 'Are

you trying to tell me that you put your baby in Mrs Dawson's pram and then pushed your own all the way home without noticing it was empty? I find that difficult to believe!'

The poor woman burst into tears. 'I don't know!' she shouted. 'I just don't know. I'm so tired I just can't think straight. I wanted this baby so badly, but now it's all gone wrong! Nobody tells you it's going to be like this!' She glared up at Maudie. 'You didn't warn me it was going to be like this, Nurse! I don't know how other women manage! That Mrs Pearson next door, she keeps telling me it will all come right when my Peggy Ann starts sleeping through the night, but she's four months old now and it hasn't happened yet. I think I'm going out of my mind, Nurse! I really think I must be going mad!'

5

'I just hope we're doing the right thing,' Dick said, shaking his head. His wife was sitting in an armchair with her feet up on a stool. Little Peggy Ann lay on her lap, sucking contentedly on a bottle of orange juice. 'I mean, you're the one who will need to get up to her if she wakes in the night. I have to get up in the morning to go to work.'

'Of course we're doing the right thing. Sheila is so deprived of sleep she doesn't know if she's coming or going. A good night's rest will work wonders. And if we can persuade her mother to come up from Cornwall for a few days, that will help too. You must admit that having a proud granny in charge will be much better for this baby than letting her go to strangers.'

'I'll still have to put in a report, mind.'

'Of course you will, love, and you'll have a better idea of what to tell your boss when you've had a word with Arthur Ramsey.'

Maudie held the baby to her shoulder and they both laughed at the enormous burp that resulted.

'Did you believe what she said, Maudie? All that business about thinking she put the child down in her own pram and wheeling it home? Even if she was so rattled that she hardly knew what she was doing, she must have realized the baby was missing when she reached the house. It sounds like a cock and bull yarn to me, or perhaps she is mentally ill, as she says. What's your take on this?'

'A bit of both, probably. It seems to me that she's suffering from post-natal depression, and that, coupled with chronic lack of sleep, has driven her almost to the breaking point. Perhaps she did lay the child down and deliberately walk away; I don't know. She certainly needs medical help.'

'And is she likely to recover from this?'

Maudie nodded. 'She'll have to see Dr Dean to have her general health assessed, and he may be able to prescribe something that will help. With some support on the home front, she may come round in time; if not, then some form of psychotherapy may be necessary. Now then, why don't you hold this little one while I try to get hold of Grandma? The sooner she gets here the better.'

Fortunately, Mary Beadle was at home when Maudie rang. 'Of course I'd love to come!' she said as soon as Maudie had given her a watered-down version of her story. 'As a matter of fact, I offered to come as soon as I had the news that little Peggy Ann had arrived, but Arthur didn't seem too keen, so I felt I couldn't insist. He's a bit of a stuffed shirt, is Arthur, and the last thing I want is to cause trouble between man and wife.'

'You leave Arthur Ramsay to me!' Maudie said grimly. 'Can I tell him when you'll be arriving? You won't want to phone the house in case you disturb Sheila while she's napping. With any luck she'll sleep round the clock.'

When arrangements had been made to Maudie's satisfaction, she hung up.

'All fixed?' Dick enquired, smoothing

baby Peggy's curls with a loving hand.

'Yes, the grandmother will be here tonight. She wanted to come before, only Arthur Ramsey headed her off at the pass, as they say in those Western films. When you interview the chap it may be as well if you let me be present, all right?'

'By the look on your face, you want to give him a few home truths,' Dick said, grinning. He knew his Maudie!

She shook her head primly. 'Not exactly, unless he drives me to it. He does need a few things explained to him, though. This is their first child, and he probably doesn't grasp all the ins and outs of how a woman feels after childbirth.'

★   ★   ★

Maudie felt her hackles rising as soon as Arthur Ramsey walked through the door. He was a rather pompous little man, obviously some years older than his wife, and he stared at the pair of them as if he had a bad smell under his nose. She knew that he was the manager of a small branch of Barclays Bank in Midvale, and he was obviously used to dealing severely with underlings.

'I understand that you have my daughter here!' he began. 'I insist you tell me what has been happening! What right do you have to keep my child from her home? I must tell you that I happen to know the Chief Constable. I shall make sure that he knows about this outrage and those responsible will be severely censured.' He glared at Dick.

'Do sit down, Mr Ramsey.' Maudie's voice was sweet. 'We have matters to discuss.'

'Matters? What matters? I don't know who you think you are, woman, but I demand you produce my daughter at once so I can take her home.'

Dick took a step forward in defence of his wife, but Maudie was equal to the occasion.

'Don't you 'woman' me, Mr Ramsey! I'm the midwife who brought your daughter into the world, as you would have known if you had been at home for the birth. Now, it's taking your wife a little time to recover, and . . . '

'If you'd done your job properly, she wouldn't be needing time to 'recover', as you put it! Childbirth is a perfectly natural event and Peggy Ann is four months old now. If there is anything wrong with my wife, she needs to pull herself together and get on with things.'

'Mr Ramsay, childbirth is a traumatic event for a woman, both physically and emotionally. Not only does labour and delivery take its toll on the mother, but the body needs time to readjust to no longer being pregnant. Most women get the 'baby blues' in the days following the birth, and in some cases post-natal depression can worsen, or persist, for weeks or months. Some women become sad and withdrawn and have trouble coping with their daily chores, and I believe this may be the case with your wife.'

'She'd better buck up, then, hadn't she!'

'It isn't that simple, Mr Ramsey. Little Peggy seems to be a colicky baby, and your wife just isn't getting the sleep she needs. Do you help by getting up in the night to see to the child so your wife can rest?'

Arthur Ramsey stared at Maudie as if she'd made an obscene remark. 'Certainly not! That's the woman's job. It may have escaped your notice, but I have a responsible job, by means of which I support the pair of them. In return, I expect my wife to provide me with a clean and comfortable home, with a hot meal waiting when I come through the door at the end of the day!'

'Queen Victoria's dead!' Maudie muttered under her breath.

'What's that? What's that you say?'

She ignored him and plunged on. 'I do understand your point of view, but it's quite plain to me that your wife needs help from some source, so I've arranged for her mother to be with you for a few weeks. She arrives tonight.'

'What!' he yelped. 'How dare you make such an arrangement without my permission? The Chief Constable shall hear of this!'

Luckily, a loud wailing came from the

bedroom at that moment, and Maudie was saved from losing her temper. 'I must see to the baby,' she said, nodding at Dick. He could take over now, and she only hoped he could explain what had transpired that day without sending the silly old fool off at the deep end. After all, the future of the Ramseys' marriage could well be at stake, and they mustn't make things worse than they already were.

★   ★   ★

'Phew!' said Dick, when Ramsey had bustled off, still complaining loudly. 'Remind me never to go to Barclays if we need a bank loan! I pity the poor devils who have to work under him, I really do.'

'And I pity his poor wife,' Maudie said. 'I only hope his mother-in-law can manage him while she's here. I wonder what on earth those two saw in each other that prompted them to get married? A lot of men still have the notion that children are women's work, but this chap's ideas are straight out of the Ark!'

'I have to congratulate you on keeping

your temper with the chap. I wouldn't have blamed you if you'd flown off the handle at him.'

'I do try to be professional, Dick!' Maudie felt rather smug. She had performed rather well under fire, hadn't she? 'If Mrs Beadle arrives tonight as planned, I'll deliver the baby to her in the morning. I'll stay long enough to make sure that Peggy is in safe hands, and then I'll leave them to it. Mind you, I'll pop in every day, just to be sure.'

'That's good. Now, all I have to do is decide what to put in my report. Let's hope that once things settle down at home, old Ramsey will change his mind about having a word with the Chief Constable! I don't want to get demoted just when I've begun my new job.'

'Don't worry. I've met his sort before. All hot air and no substance. 'A personal friend of the Chief Constable', my eye! I expect the Chief Constable is just a customer at the bank, and our Arthur only knows him to bow and scrape to. That's what it will be.'

'I hope you're right,' Dick muttered.

6

Maudie and Dick strolled down to the Royal Oak, enjoying the Saturday morning sunshine. There was a nip in the air and some of the leaves were already beginning to change colour.

'I could have made lunch at home, you know,' Maudie murmured, feeling slightly guilty at the thought of paying out good money for bread and cheese and a pickled onion when she had all those items in her larder. She had been on her own for so long, making every sixpence do the work of a shilling, that it was hard to give up her old thrifty ways. Not that she could afford to go mad now, of course, but it did make a difference having two wage packets coming in.

'You deserve a break, love,' Dick said. 'Washing windows is hard work, and I've been too busy on those reports to give you a hand. Never mind, I'm up-to-date now, so we may as well go out and enjoy ourselves.' Maudie was not about to argue with that!

The bar of the Royal Oak was quiet, with just a few regulars sitting over their pints. Two men sat in one corner, intent on their game of dominoes, with a shaggy dog stretched out at their feet. Behind the bar, landlord Len Frost was busy polishing glasses with a red-and-white-checked cloth.

'How do, Nurse, Sarge! What'll be?'

'Ale for me and a shandy for the missus, please,' Dick replied. 'And we'll have a bite of bread and cheese while we're here.'

'Right you are. Coming right up. Two Ploughman's, Dora!' the landlord called back over his shoulder. An answering murmur from an inner room signified that his wife had heard him.

'And how is married life treating you, Nurse?' he asked, handing Maudie her shandy. 'A lady of leisure now, are you?'

'Not exactly, Len,' Maudie told him. 'I'm still doing the local midwifery, and I'm busy enough at home these days. All that keeps me hopping.'

'Ah, there's some as wishes you was still doing the regular nursing around the district. It's not the same with that Nurse Gregg, not by a long chalk.'

'Why, what's the matter with her?' Dick wondered. Maudie was glad that he'd asked. Of course she was dying to know what the new nurse had been up to, but professional etiquette forbade her to indulge in open criticism of a colleague.

Len leaned forward, lowering his voice. 'It seems there's been complaints that people can't get hold of her when she's wanted. Nobody has telephones over at the prefabs where she stays, so folks have to ring the newsagent's on the corner, and he sends a message down. And most of them have to find a telephone kiosk in the first place, so trying to get in touch with the nurse is a tricky business.'

'That doesn't sound good,' Dick agreed.

Maudie felt she had to say something in defence of the way things worked. She was proud of her reputation when it came to providing superb health care for patients, and she didn't want it said that standards were slipping as soon as a new nurse came on the scene.

'People are well aware that they have various options in case of emergency,' she reminded them. 'They can dial 999 for an ambulance, or telephone Dr Dean directly. And the nurse is supposed to hold regular clinics at the surgery, just as I used to do. If there are any problems, I'm sure they'll be ironed out as soon as the people get used to Nurse Gregg's ways.'

'Ah, but that's it!' Len said, shaking his head. 'There's been times when she's never turned up for home visits. There's been people waiting in all morning and she's never come. Take Lily Dobb, for instance. You know she looks after her old Dad, him as had the stroke a while back. Well, last week, there she was, waiting for Nurse to pop in and give her a hand lifting the old boy so she could change his sheets. She waited and waited and Nurse never come. Well, I know what that's like, you can't get started on nothing else, so you stand around looking at the clock, getting crosser and crosser.'

'Obviously something must have come up,' Maudie said. 'Some emergency that Nurse had to deal with. And of course the Dobbs aren't on the phone, so she couldn't let them know she'd been delayed.'

'Delayed, is it! Huh! She never showed up at all, and poor old Ben was left lying in a puddle till Lily's man got home from work to help her.'

'What do you make of that, then?' Dick asked, when he and Maudie were seated at a table for two, with their food in front of them. 'Falling down on the job, is she?'

Maudie shrugged. 'Hard to say. It may be she's getting lost on the way to some of those remote farms. All the old signposts were removed during the war, of course, and most of them have never been replaced. Well, people who have lived here all their lives know where everything is, so what's the point? Council have better things to do with their money than to label every little byway.'

'Surely somebody could have shown the girl what was what,' Dick mumbled through a mouthful of crusty bread.

Maudie glared at him. 'I offered to go with the silly creature on her rounds when she first came, but she made it quite clear that she didn't want any interference from me! Well, she can jolly well stew in her own juice from now on, and it won't worry me if she falls flat on her face!'

'That's a bit hard on the patients who need her in a hurry, isn't it?' Dick protested, squelching his way through a juicy pickled onion.

'As I pointed out, they can always dial 999 in an emergency. Every schoolchild knows that. It sounds to me as if the problem lies with the ordinary home visits, and that side of things is no longer any of my business since I married a gorgeous hunk of a man with film-star good looks!'

'Fool!' Dick said, going pink round the ears. 'But shouldn't you do something about this? Put a word in Dr Dean's ear, for instance?'

'Not unless somebody comes to me directly with a complaint. You know what you've told me about hearsay not being evidence? The same thing applies here. I say, do you want that last bit of cheese, or can I have it?'

★ ★ ★

Two days later Maudie made her way to the Ramseys' house, being careful to arrive well after the charming Arthur had left for the bank. Monday mornings were difficult enough without running into a patient's belligerent husband.

She was greeted by Mary Beadle, a neatly dressed fiftyish woman with a beaming smile.

'Do come in, Nurse! I've got the kettle on, and I'm sure you won't say no to a cup of tea! Or do you prefer coffee? It's only Camp, I'm afraid, but I can make it with boiled milk.'

'I'd love a cup of tea, please. And how are things here this morning?'

'Both Sheila and the baby have had a good night, I'm happy to say.'

'And Mr Ramsey?'

Mrs Beadle pulled a face. 'I'm afraid

he's part of the problem! If I hear him say just one more time that having a baby is natural, and all Sheila has to do is pull up her socks and get on with it, I shall scream!'

'I have tried to explain to him the part that hormones play in pregnancy and motherhood, but he can't seem to take it in.'

'Doesn't want to, you mean! Silly old fool. Well, I'm here now, and I can act as a buffer between them if need be. Not that it will be easy. He's already treating me like some kind of housemaid, giving me orders and turning up his nose at the good food I put in front of him.'

'How long do you expect to stay, Mrs Beadle?'

'Do call me Mary. Well, as long as it takes, really.'

'There's nothing pressing at home, then?'

'No, no. I'm a widow, as perhaps you're aware, and fortunately my late husband left me well fixed so I don't need to hold down a job. I do a lot of voluntary work, of course, and I sit on a number of committees, but they can manage without me for a few weeks. Nobody is indispensable!'

'I'm sure Sheila is glad to have you here.'

'Actually, I wanted to talk to you about that. As I said, I can stay as long as she needs me, but I'm thinking of taking her and the baby down to Cornwall with me. It's lovely there at this time of year, and a change of scene will do her the world of good. The thing is, I've heard about her bit of trouble from Arthur, and I want to know if she'll be allowed to leave Llandyfan. Are there any charges pending? And what about little Peggy Ann? Arthur said something about a foster home, and I do so hope that situation has been resolved.'

'I can find out for you. My husband is the detective in charge of the case.' Maudie felt a thrill as she uttered the magical words 'my husband'. And she was proud of Dick's recent promotion, too! 'I can't make any promises, because the decision may rest with someone higher up, but if I'm asked I shall certainly recommend that the baby should be released into your care. And speaking of Peggy Ann, may I have a look at her now? It's just a formality, but I'd like to be able to report that she's safe and well.'

'Of course,' Mary said, getting up to lead the way to the front room, where the little girl was lying in her cot. Maudie followed in her wake, confident that the baby was in good hands.

7

'We've had that banker chap in here, boasting about being a good pal of the Chief Constable and threatening us with all sorts,' DI Goodwood informed Dick.

'I was afraid of that, sir. I can assure you that everything was done by the book.'

'He's implying that you took his daughter away without his permission, Bryant.'

Dick's neck reddened. 'Hardly that, sir! That is, no, I didn't have his say-so because he didn't know a thing about it. As you know, I was called to the scene, where I found the baby apparently abandoned. I had to take charge of her for her own protection.'

'Quite. Experienced with babies, are you, Bryant?'

'Not exactly, sir, but it so happens that my wife is the local midwife, and I handed little Peggy Ann over to her right away. In fact, it was Maudie who was able to identify her, on account of having delivered the child when she was born.'

'Handy, that.'

'Yes, sir. And it was my wife who contacted the grandmother and got her to come up from Cornwall to look after things at the house.'

'Which, so I'm told, doesn't sit well with the proud father!'

Dick sighed. 'There seems to be no pleasing the man either way. He won't do anything to help his wife with the baby — says that's women's work — yet he doesn't want his mother-in-law on the spot either. My wife has been to the house to check on things, and apparently this Mrs Beadle wants to take her daughter and the baby back to Cornwall for a bit, until young Mrs Ramsey gets her strength back. Do you think that's possible, in view of the charge of child abandonment that's pending?'

'That will be for the magistrate to decide, Bryan. Oh, it won't come up in open court, but I've had a word with the social worker, and she's made an appointment for you with Mrs Furey to discuss the situation. You're to go along at ten-thirty.'

'Right you are, sir. Will do.'

* * *

Dick phoned home to discuss this with Maudie. 'I'm not sure what to say to the woman, really, love. Oh, I can give her the facts, but I'm afraid I'll drop your Mrs Ramsey right in it. It should be you doing this, really.'

'All you have to do is to quote me on the subject, Dick. Sheila Ramsey is not a bad person or an unloving mother. I'm quite sure she's suffering from post-natal depression, and that, coupled with sleep deprivation due to a colicky baby, caused a temporary loss of control. I've already mentioned the problem to Dr Dean, and Mrs Beadle has agreed to take Sheila to see him. I'm quite sure the situation will right itself in time.'

'And your recommendation is that she be allowed to go down to Cornwall in her mother's care?'

'Absolutely. Dr Dean can have a word

with Mrs Beadle's doctor there, and if the magistrate isn't happy with the arrangement, she can always arrange for them to have regular visits from a social worker locally.'

'Right ho. See you later, then. Unless something unforeseen crops up I shouldn't be late back this evening.'

'Lamb cutlets and minty peas for tea.'

'Lovely! Ta-ta!'

*   *   *

Mrs Furey was a grey-haired, grandmotherly type of woman, dressed in a pale blue cashmere twin set, a Gor-Ray skirt and pearls. She listened patiently as Dick stumbled through his carefully prepared speech, occasionally making a note on a miniature clipboard.

'In essence, then, your view is that young Mrs Ramsey is more sinned against than sinning.'

'Er, yes, I suppose so. I mean, there's no denying she left the baby outside the vicarage and walked away, but I do believe she was temporarily out of her mind, and so not responsible.'

'Quite. The crux of the matter is whether she is competent to care for her child now, or if other arrangements need to be made.'

'The grandmother seems a sensible sort of person,' Dick said, hoping he hadn't put his foot in it with those damning words 'out of her mind'. He hadn't meant that the way it sounded. 'My wife has been to see her, and has summed her up as being just what Mrs Ramsey needs at the moment. Surely it is better for the child to remain in her grandmother's care than to go among strangers?'

'And your wife is a qualified nurse; is that correct?'

'She is the local midwife. In fact, she knows the situation better than anyone because she actually delivered the baby, you know.'

Mrs Furey looked at him over the top of her spectacles. 'Then I'm surprised that she didn't anticipate this situation developing. I expect that post-natal visits must have taken place?'

'I'm sure she's done her best,' Dick

muttered, dismayed by this criticism of his beloved Maudie. He bit his lip. It would only sound like a weak excuse if he tried to explain that Maudie had been off-duty while getting married, going on honeymoon, and then having her work schedule rearranged. Nor was this the time to point out that his wife had been embroiled in mayhem and murder in the recent past, from which she had been lucky to escape with her life!

The magistrate looked down at her notes with an expression of distaste on her aristocratic face. 'I have received a letter from the child's father, Mr Arthur Ramsey,' she said. 'I cannot say that I'm in sympathy with his views.'

'Oh?'

'He seems to be suggesting that if his wife will pull herself together, as he has repeatedly instructed her to do, matters will quickly get back to normal and the unfortunate episode that took place at the vicarage can be forgotten. He further suggests that Mrs Mary Beadle should be instructed to return to Cornwall forthwith, since she is encouraging his wife to 'slack off', as he puts it.'

'Stone the crows!' Dick muttered under his breath.

'What was that, Detective Sergeant?'

'Er, nothing, milady. I meant, I hope they don't come to blows.'

'As to that, I'd rather like to box the fellow's ears!' Mrs Furey announced, suddenly appearing quite human. 'Apart from the fact that post-natal depression is a well-known medical condition, and certainly not the fault of anyone who is unfortunate enough to suffer from it, the man is like something out of the Dark Ages! Who on earth does he think he is? Silly old buffer!'

Dick grinned. 'I know I wouldn't care to work for him at the bank.'

'My thoughts exactly. Therefore, I've decided that the charges against Mrs Ramsey shall be dismissed, and that the baby Peggy Ann Ramsey shall remain with her, under the continuing supervision of Mrs Mary Beadle.'

'And what about their application to go to Mrs Beadle's home in Cornwall?'

'Granted, on condition that Mrs

Ramsey receives appropriate medical care. Now, then, is there anything more to discuss, Mr Bryant?'

'Er . . . Arthur Ramsey is threatening to report us to the Chief Constable,' Dick said, greatly daring.

'And you are afraid the result will be a black mark on your record.' A lovely smile broke over the magistrate's face. 'I think you can safely leave the Chief Constable to me, Detective Sergeant. Clive Marshall is my cousin, and I grew up knowing how to manage him!'

★ ★ ★

'So that's how it turned out,' Dick told Maudie that night. He had enjoyed the promised lamb cutlets, followed by sticky toffee pudding, and was now stretched out in his armchair in his stockinged feet. 'The old girl was really quite human.'

'So I should hope. She's probably a mother too, and even if she's never experienced full-blown depression herself, she must remember what it felt like to have the baby blues. Or how it feels to suddenly find yourself caring for a helpless infant, whose very existence depends on you.'

'So the upshot is, Mrs Beadle can take Sheila and Peggy Ann to Cornwall, and old Arthur will just have to lump it.'

'Do him good to manage on his own for a bit, although I doubt he'll really appreciate what his wife does for him when she is there. It's a bit of luck Mrs Furey being the Chief Constable's cousin, though, isn't it? That should keep Arthur Ramsey off your back.'

'And I'm jolly glad about that!' Dick said. 'I really didn't want to get sent back to uniform when I've only just been promoted.'

'Oh, it would never have gone that far, surely? You behaved perfectly correctly, Dick. In fact, I don't see what else you could have done, given the circumstances.'

'Maybe not, but I didn't want to find myself in the middle of a brouhaha quite this soon.'

'Never mind, all's well that end's well,' Maudie said, getting up to give him a kiss.

8

As summer moved towards autumn, life for Maudie and Dick settled into a routine. Dick was busy with a case on the other side of the county that involved a particularly unpleasant fraud.

★   ★   ★

A large number of people had made down-payments on building lots in what had turned out to be a nonexistent housing development. Repeated enquiries as to when building would start had come to nothing, until at last the police had been asked to look into it.

'As it turns out, the developer doesn't even own the land,' Dick told Maudie. 'It's part of an abandoned property that nobody quite knows what to do with now that that the farmer has passed on. His wife is in a nursing home, quite senile, poor dear, and the son is believed to be somewhere in South Africa but can't be traced.'

'I hope they won't be sending you over there to track him down, then!'

'Oh, no, love. That side of things has nothing to do with us. No, we're trying to catch up with this Mitchell Mills, the developer. It seems he found out somehow that this land is unoccupied and he started advertising lots for sale, knowing that nobody was likely to pop up and ask him what he thought he was up to.'

'But could he do that? I mean, don't you have to prove ownership before you can get planning permission?'

'Anyone can get a fancy brochure printed, love. And that, apparently, is just what he did. He collected some hefty down-payments, handed them some equally dodgy documents in return, and sailed off into the sunset. He really sold them a pup!'

'At least nobody died,' Maudie murmured, thinking back over the murders they had experienced in recent years in Llandyfan.

'You wouldn't dismiss it so lightly if you heard some of the stories that have been told to me. You know what it's been like after the war, Maudie. People living any old how, no affordable housing available, and no hope of moving up the waiting list to build because materials are in such short supply. Young couples starting married life in one bedroom of their parents' house, or several generations all squashed together in close quarters.'

'All right, all right! You can get down off your soap-box! I've seen some sights in my job that would make your hair curl, too.'

'I'm sorry, love. Didn't mean to preach. It's just that this Mills chap makes my blood boil! He's trampled all over people's hopes and dreams, and now they're worse off than they were before because he's scarpered with their savings.'

'Do you think you'll catch up with him?'

'We'll have a jolly good try, but as for recovering any of the money he's stolen, I doubt we'll ever see a penny. It's a nasty case, Maudie.'

★   ★   ★

For her part, Maudie carried on as usual, delivering the occasional baby, and performing ante- and post-natal care for the mothers in her charge. The gossip-mongers had by now squeezed the last ounce of excitement out of her narrow escape from death at the hands of the fake Dr Ransome, prior to her wedding, and they were casting about for new topics of conversation.

'Is it true about that bank manager's wife trying to do away with her poor baby?' an expectant mother asked when she had cornered Maudie in her little office in the parish hall. She patted her stomach. 'Ooh, I hope I don't go all funny when this one comes. You never know, do you?'

'Just roll up your sleeve, will you please, Mrs Povey?' Maudie asked, getting out the sphygmomanometer ready to take the woman's blood pressure.

'Where on earth did you hear such nonsense?'

'Oh, it's not nonsense, Nurse! It's all over the village. Mrs Dawson's been telling everybody, and she should know. It was her pram the little girl was left in.'

'I might have known!' Maudie said, with a sigh. 'Mrs Ramsey was worn out with the baby crying, and she just put her down for a moment in a safe place while she walked around for a bit to give herself a break.' It was a gross exaggeration, of course, but Maudie felt it necessary to nip this in the bud. Presumably poor Sheila Ramsey would have to come back to Llandyfan sooner or later, and she could do without silly talk like this.

Jenny Povey made a rude noise with her lips, prompting Maudie to continue firmly: 'And it was unfortunate that, before Sheila could come back for the baby, Mrs Dawson came out of the vicarage and found the wrong baby in her pram. She made a very silly fuss and the vicar felt he had to call for help. If only Mrs Blunt had been at home at the time, none of this would have happened.'

'Really!'

'Yes, really! And I was there, so I know what I'm talking about. And I can't discuss my other patients with you, Mrs Povey, so can we change the subject, please?'

Maudie unwrapped the blood-pressure cuff from her patient's arm and made a note on her chart. After dispensing a few words of wisdom about diet, exercise and the need for rest, she smiled reassuringly at the young woman. 'Everything is going along as it should, Mrs Povey. Is there anything you'd like to ask me while you're here? Otherwise I'll see you again in a month.'

The young woman leaned forward, frowning. 'Will it be you, Nurse, or that other one?'

'I don't quite understand. Will what be me?'

'Will it be you that brings the baby?' For one wild moment Maudie wondered if the girl was expecting her to arrive at the house with the infant in her black bag, as many youngsters were led to believe, but she realized it was just a figure of speech.

'Well, yes, I expect it will be me. I am your midwife, you know,' she said.

'Oh, that's all right, then. I thought you might be sort of retiring now you're a married woman. I was afraid it might be that one that's stopping at the prefabs.'

'If you mean Nurse Gregg, she hasn't done her midwifery training. She's come here to do general nursing in the district.'

'That's if she turns up when she's supposed to. I didn't want her leaving me in the lurch when I'm in labour. I'm scared enough as it is!'

'There's nothing to be afraid of,' Maudie said soothingly. 'Delivering a baby is hard work, but you'll be safe with me. I'll be with you every step of the way. You can count on that.'

'But things do go wrong sometimes, I know they do! I read about some of the awful things that can happen in a magazine at the hairdresser's. There was this woman on an island in the Hebrides, or was it the Scilly Isles? Everything started to happen at once, and . . .'

'You live half a mile outside the village,' Maudie told her, chuckling. 'And if you did happen to need extra help, then whatever may be required is readily available. That's why we have ambulances and the cottage hospital.'

'I know, but if it was that Nurse Gregg and she didn't come . . . '

Maudie felt herself torn two ways. It wasn't the thing to discuss a colleague's failings with outsiders; and, as she had said to Dick, it wasn't her place to investigate possible misdemeanors unless a patient approached her directly. Let them go through the proper channels by speaking to Dr Dean or Councillor Reeves. Only now it seemed as if little Mrs Povey was trying to get something off her chest. Shouldn't Maudie at least listen to what she had to say?

'Has Nurse Gregg let you down in some way?' she began carefully. 'She is fairly new to the area, you know, and it may be that she has had trouble finding her way about.'

'Not me; not yet. I haven't given her the chance. But there's plenty who could tell you a different story.'

'Such as?'

'Well, like my neighbour, Mrs Hobbs. Her hubby has a bad chest, and the nurse promised to stop in and show her how to make a special poultice. An 'Auntie Flo' I think she called it. Mrs Hobbs makes bread poultices to bring her old man's boils to a head, but the nurse said no, this is something different.'

'Antiphlogistine,' I expect, Maudie said.

'Maybe. Anyway, Mrs Hobbs stayed in all day with the old man, and him all dressed up in his best pajamas, and the nurse never come.'

'Dear me.'

'And as for young Bobby Andrews' mummy, well! She didn't know where to put herself after that nurse tore a strip off her in front of everyone in the waiting room!'

'What was that all about?'

'He was running a temperature, and we don't have a doctor here no more to make house calls, so she took him up the surgery. Nurse Gregg takes a look at him and she says as Bobby has the measles, and his mother should have never have brought him there, spreading all his germs around for everybody to catch.

'How was I supposed to know he'd caught the measles?' Mrs Andrews says. 'You're the nurse, not me. Why d'you think I brought him up here?'

'You should have noticed the Koplik's spots, Mother,' says that young madam.

'What's one of them when it's at home?' Mrs Andrews bawls. 'And don't you call me Mother!' Mrs Andrews walks out in a huff with poor young Bobby behind her, crying his eyes out. What do you think of that, then, Nurse Bryant, eh? I told you it was bad.'

'Don't you worry about a thing,' Maudie said. 'I'll be with you when your time comes, and all will be well. In the meantime, you trot along home and put your feet up. Don't forget to come back in a month, and try to keep your weight gain down to just a few pounds every few weeks. A total gain of about twenty pounds by the end of the pregnancy is what we have to aim for.'

When her patient had gone, Maudie leaned over her desk with her chin on her hands. Even allowing for exaggeration, it sounded as if Nurse Melanie Gregg needed talking to. It looked as if Maudie was the person who had to tackle that, and she wasn't looking forward to it!

9

The following afternoon found Maudie sitting at the kitchen table, leafing through her cookery books. The local gamekeeper had presented her with a fine rabbit that morning, and she wanted to do it justice.

She had delivered all five of his children back in the days before the National Health Service came into being, and he had always paid her in kind. Sometimes a selection of vegetables from his prize-winning garden plot, and on one memorable occasion a fat hen that his wife had raised from a day-old chick. Far from being a disappointment, these items had been worth their weight in gold during those wartime years when food was strictly rationed.

'My goodness, just look at this!' Maudie said, looking at the rabbit with admiration. 'Have I delivered a new baby for you and forgotten all about it? I must be going dotty in my old age.'

'No, no, Nurse,' he told her. 'She's finished with all that, the missus has. Got the change of life, see?'

'Then to what do I owe this fine specimen, Mr Parsons?'

He favoured her with a gap-toothed grin. 'It's a wedding present, innit? Just to say we ain't forgot what you done for us, like.'

'Well, thank you very much indeed! I'm sure my husband will enjoy a bit of rabbit.'

'Aye, that's right. The way to a chap's heart is through his stomach, eh?'

Now it was decision time. With any luck, she could stretch this for three meals; now the weather was a bit cooler, the food would keep well on the marble shelf in the larder. She thought of making a pie; that would do for this evening, and then a stew for the remaining two days . . .

The problem was that she had never made a rabbit stew before, and she wasn't sure if the method was similar to an Irish stew. Were you supposed to include vegetables in it, or simply cook it in a rich gravy, serving cabbage or something separately?

The telephone rang, making her jump. She was pleased to hear Dick's voice on the other end of the line.

'Everything all right, is it?' she asked, when they had exchanged greetings.

'Right as rain, love. The thing is, I won't be able to get home tonight, and possibly not tomorrow either.'

'Oh? Where are you, then?'

'Neath.'

'Neath in Wales? Glamorganshire?'

'I don't know of any other Neath.'

'But why? That's a long way from your area, Dick.'

'Hm. Well, you remember that Mills fellow I told you about? He's been nabbed by the force down here, and the boss and I have come to interview him. Apparently he's been staying with a sister here, and that's why it's taken so long to trace him.'

'I'm glad they've caught him, but surely he could have been returned here, where he committed his crimes?'

'It looks as if this business may have been more widespread than we originally thought. He might have been conning people in other places as well; he could even be part of a larger crime ring. So, as I said, I may not be home for a day or two. Will you be all right on your own, love? Do you want me to ring Mrs Blunt and see if she can come and stay with you?'

Maudie laughed. 'For goodness' sake, Dick Bryant! I've lived here on my own for donkey's years. I'm not about to get the vapours now!'

He chuckled. 'Of course you have, love! I wasn't thinking. Whoops! There go the pips! See you when I see you, then! Love you!'

'Love you too,' Maudie told him, but he was gone.

★ ★ ★

Maudie decided to postpone the decision about the rabbit until the next morning. It would be safe enough hanging in the larder, and she would cook something

84

simple for herself for tea. What she really fancied was a hot crumpet, dripping with butter, but it wasn't the season for them so that was a non-starter. The thought of Wales made her think of Welsh rarebit, which of course wasn't rabbit at all, but cheese on toast. Yes, she would have that, unless Dick had polished off all the cheese. He had a habit of wandering into the larder at odd times to make himself a little snack, and when it came to cheese he had all the instincts of a great big mouse.

She had nothing planned for the evening, so perhaps she should have an early night; hop into bed with the new Agatha Christie she had managed to get from the library. She had been feeling weary lately and she didn't know why. Too much on her mind, probably. This business of Nurse Gregg was getting her down, and she was putting off the evil moment when she had to do something about it.

The problem was that she wasn't the girl's supervisor, and so it wasn't really her place to take her to task. They were co-workers in parallel jobs. Yet if half the tales about her were true, she must be spoken to, for the sake of the patients in her care. But Maudie didn't fancy a stand-off, particularly when she hadn't observed any lack of care herself but had only received complaints at second, even third-hand.

The obvious choice seemed to be going through official channels, but that would mean speaking to Councillor Reeves, and Maudie and the pompous pharmacist had never quite seen eye-to-eye on medical matters. He was known to have an eye for pretty young assistants, and no doubt he would succumb to Nurse Gregg's charms if she simpered at him in response to his jovial remarks. He would interpret Maudie's complaints as professional jealousy and dismiss them out of hand. Well, blow the pair of them! She would leave the problem for another day and instead immerse herself in the world of Hercule Poirot, where everything was neatly solved by using the little grey cells.

But somehow the novel failed to engage Maudie's attention, and she pushed it aside impatiently. Why was she so weary? Was she coming down with a cold or something? Or was she undergoing a reaction to her change in circumstances? She had read somewhere that any major lifestyle change — even a positive one — might cause stress on the body, and of course she was newly-married.

Could that be it? Dick was a wonderful husband: considerate, thoughtful, a tender lover. Yet having another person about the place after living alone for so long was certainly an adjustment. No more shrugging herself into a comfortable old dressing-gown in the morning, and downing two cups of tea before doing anything else. Now she had to comb her hair and put on lipstick before Dick so much as opened his eyes. She wasn't a girl of twenty any more, and she couldn't let him think he'd married a fright!

And then there was the housewife thing. Dick had to be fed properly. For Maudie there could be no more dashing in from work and having a boiled egg or beans on toast on a tray. A man wanted meat and potatoes, and a good pudding!

And there were other things. Washing, ironing, mending. When she came to think about it, Maudie had had little to do with all that over the years. She had always worn a uniform of one sort of another, starting with a regulation gymslip at the council school. The hospitals where she'd worked had provided the uniform dresses, aprons and caps, all of which had been washed and starched in the hospital laundry and sent to the sewing room if mending was required. Now, she still wore uniforms to work, and possessed very few garments which she thought of as 'civvies'.

But now she also had Dick to consider, and quite naturally he expected his wife to keep him in clean shirts and carefully-darned socks. She was happy to perform these small services, which seemed to her like an act of love. In fact, she was still at the stage where all these wifely activities had a feeling of pride and achievement attached to them. No doubt the novelty would soon wear off! Still, she accepted her new status gladly, and was pleased to have the opportunity to look after her husband's needs.

She did hope that she could soon shake off this weary feeling, though. Surely getting married couldn't call for such a big adjustment as all that? It had to be something else. Perhaps she was approaching the menopause. She did hope she could sail through that without the difficulties that some women experienced. In fact, she was rather looking forward to it. She would be glad to be finished with all that other business.

'Oh, do stop drivelling on, Maudie Bryant!' she said aloud. 'Count your blessings! You've got a good husband, a good home, a job you love and a comfortable bed to rest your weary bones in. Just roll over and go to sleep. Tomorrow is another day.'

Conjuring up Dick's homely face in her mind's eye, she planted a goodnight kiss on his rugged cheek and hoped he was thinking of her. She put her head on Dick's pillow, imagining he was there. She closed her eyes, and slept.

10

Like so many others who turned to the vicar's wife in time of trouble, Maudie went to chat to her friend Joan Blunt. She needed to clarify her thinking on what she should do about Melanie Gregg; or, to get right down to it, Melanie Gregg's attitude.

' . . . and so there it is,' she concluded. 'Do you think I'm being a fusspot?'

'Of course not, Nurse. I realize it's a delicate situation, but on the other hand you have a responsibility to the people in the parish if there really is something wrong. You'd never forgive yourself if somebody suffered through that young woman's negligence and you hadn't done your utmost to prevent it. Mind you, people do grumble over the slightest things, particularly where mis-understandings are involved. It's only human nature, I suppose. Is there any possibility that Mrs Dawson, to quote one example, is making a mountain out of a molehill?'

'I suppose there could be a rational explanation about the missed appointments. Being new to the district, Nurse Gregg may have got lost or delayed along the way; it could happen to anyone. But in that case she should have explained herself to the patients and apologized.'

'And do we know that she didn't do that?'

'Well, no. All we have is Ella Dawson's word for what went on.'

'I see.'

'But what riles me up is the way she treats people,' Maudie burst out. 'She has a most unfortunate manner. She almost bit my head off when I offered to show her around the district; and as for scolding young Bobby's mother because she brought him to the surgery with measles, that was quite uncalled-for, for more reasons than one.'

'I expect she's feeling unsure of herself in a new situation, don't you think?'

Maudie shook her head. 'Begging your pardon, Mrs Blunt, but you've never been a nurse so you don't understand how these things work. When a girl goes into training, she very soon learns that she must show respect for her superiors, or she'll find herself on the carpet in Matron's office. And I don't just mean deferring to the ward sisters! She must show respect to girls even one set ahead of her own: standing aside to let them precede her into the lift, waiting until they are seated at meals before taking her own place, and so on.'

'That sounds a bit severe.'

'It's all part of hospital discipline. We all find it hard to come to terms with it at first, until we come to understand that it's necessary to be able to face any difficulty that may arise, such as keeping calm and carrying on in an emergency.'

'Like soldiers being prepared to go into battle.'

'Exactly. What I'm trying to say is that I'd have expected Nurse Gregg to treat me with a bit of the professional courtesy due to a senior colleague, even if privately she feels that I'm interfering.' A thought struck Maudie.

'I say, I suppose she is a properly-qualified nurse? I mean, somebody on the committee did look into her credentials?'

Mrs Blunt laughed. 'Don't tell me you think we've got another imposter on our hands? Just because Dr Ransome turned out to be a con man, it doesn't mean there's something fishy about Nurse Gregg!'

'I know! I know! Don't mind me. I expect she's just a silly little girl who's worked her way free from hospital discipline and is determined to rule the roost in her new job. That doesn't alter the fact that patients are falling through the cracks, and I don't know what to do about it. I simply cannot drop in on somebody else's patients and ask them if they have any complaints! So what on earth are we going to do?'

Mrs Blunt thought for a moment and then clapped her hands, looking delighted. 'Harold!' she announced.

'Harold?'

'My husband, of course! It's part of his job to call on the sick and shut-ins. We'll let him in on the problem, and he can keep his ears open when he's on his rounds.'

'Send him to snoop on Nurse Gregg, you mean.'

Joan Blunt looked at Maudie over the top of her spectacles. 'That isn't worthy of you, Nurse.'

Maudie grinned. 'Perhaps not, but the end result will be the same. All right, then. Wind him up and get him going. We can't let this situation drag on much longer.'

* * *

Maudie returned to her cottage, feeling much better. She was glad that Mrs Blunt had offered to speak to the vicar on her behalf. The thought of getting him involved had already occurred to her, although she was glad to let Mrs Blunt think it was her own idea. The vicar tended to be unworldly at times, and Maudie suspected that if she confided in him about Nurse Gregg's shortcomings he might have said something about casting out the mote in her own eye. And wasn't that what clergymen were for, seeing the best in people whenever possible, but rooting out sin where they found it lurking?

Having come into the cottage by the back entrance she was startled to hear an agonized thumping on the front door. She hastened to open it and found a wild-eyed man on the step with his fist raised ready to knock again.

'Yes? Can I help you?'

'Are you the nurse? I thought I'd never find you! I've been here twice and you weren't home, and then I went up the surgery and there's nobody there, and I can't call 999 because I don't have any change for the phone box, and . . . '

'I'm here now,' Maudie said, in the soothing voice she used for expectant fathers. 'I don't think I know your name. Is it a midwife you need, or an everyday nurse?'

'Yes! No, I mean, both. How do I know? It's my wife, Jenny.'

'Ah, you must be Mr Povey, then. I'm the midwife, Nurse Bryant. I'll come at once. Can you tell me what the problem is? Is your wife having pains?'

'She's yelling a lot.'

'And have you noticed any blood at all?'

The man frowned. 'I don't think so. Should there be?'

Maudie hurried down the village street with Povey loping along at her side. His panic seemed to have subsided but he seemed incapable of recounting what had really happened, except that he had come in from work, expecting to find his dinner on the table, and had found his wife 'just lying there'. He had put a cushion under her head and dashed off to find help.

Maudie hoped that the girl wasn't about to miscarry this much-wanted first child. At four months there was no hope of its survival if the fetus came away now.

Jenny Povey was lying on the bathroom floor and she was very cross indeed. 'Where have you been all this time, Tom Povey, you great lummox!' she bawled. 'I came in here because I want to go to the loo and I can't get up!'

Maudie carried out a swift examination and found, to her relief, that the girl wasn't in labour and that the baby's heartbeat was steady and strong, if a little fast.

'Can you tell me what happened to you, dear?'

Jenny rolled her eyes. 'Didn't Tom say? I came in here to the loo and there must have been a bit of water on the floor. I'd been cleaning the bath earlier and I expect I spilled some. My feet went from under me and I went down on my bottom. And ouch, did that hurt! I was afraid to try to get up in case I'd broken my back, so I sent Tom for help.' Tears began to seep down her flushed cheeks.

Maudie was quick to reassure her. By the way that Jenny was kicking her feet petulantly at her husband, there wasn't much wrong with her spinal cord.

Rolling the girl onto her side, she prodded her gently. 'I think you probably broke your coccyx — your tailbone — when you sat down hard on the tile floor. There's nothing to worry about; it doesn't serve a useful purpose. I shall ask Dr Dean to make a house call to confirm the diagnosis, but I'm pretty sure that's what you've done.'

'Shouldn't she go to the hospital, Nurse?' Tom Povey was calm now and in control of himself. 'They'll want to put her in a plaster cast, won't they?'

Maudie smiled. 'There's no need for anything like that, Mr Povey. The bone will heal by itself, given time. I'm afraid you won't feel like sitting down for a while, though, Jenny. You'll have to eat reclining on your side, like a wealthy Roman matron. And now, Mr Povey, you must help me get your wife to her feet, or there will be another puddle on the floor before we know it. I'll show you what to do. Ups-a-daisy!'

Some time later Maudie took her leave, accompanied to the gate by Tom Povey, who was full of apologies for his previous confusion. 'I didn't know what sort of nurse was wanted, you see. I thought she might have broken something, and that would need one sort of nurse, wouldn't it? But if it was the baby, then she needed a midwife.'

Maudie patted him on the back. 'That's quite all right, Mr Povey. You did the right thing. When you weren't able to dial 999, any nurse at all would have steered you right. We're all trained to know what to do in case of an emergency.'

And I jolly well hope that's true if one of my expectant mothers happens to run into Nurse Gregg, she thought grimly.

11

Dick returned from Neath, feeling disgruntled.

'What were you doing down there all this time?' Maudie asked him.

'Searching his sister's house for evidence. We needed proof of what the blighter has been up to in his dealings with the poor souls he's defrauded.'

'And did you come up with anything useful?'

'Luckily, yes. He's kept meticulous records, as it happens. Turns out that he used to be an accountant in another life. Your friend Arthur Ramsey would be proud of his book-keeping.'

'That's good, isn't it?'

'Well, it will certainly help the prosecution when his case comes to trial, but it won't do much for his victims. There isn't a trace of the money he's collected, and if it isn't found there's not a hope of them ever seeing any of their money again.'

'That's a rotten shame! Will you have to go back to Neath now?'

'No, we've finished our investigation there, and Mills has been transferred up here to await trial.'

'That's good. I've missed you!'

Dick took her into his arms and for a few minutes neither of them spoke. Then Maudie pulled herself free to attend to a saucepan that was in danger of boiling over on the stove. 'So what's next for you?' she called back over her shoulder. 'Any chance of us getting away for a day or two? I'd love to go somewhere far away from Llandyfan, where nobody's ever heard of Miss Melanie Gregg!'

'You sound a bit fed up, love. What's the matter? Work getting you down?'

'Oh, I don't know. I've been feeling a bit under the weather, that's all.'

'Have you been doing too much? You come and sit down over here and put your feet up, and I'll make you a nice cup of tea. And you know, if going out to work delivering babies and looking after me is all too much, you can always give up the job and stay home. We can quite well manage on my salary alone, especially now I've been promoted.'

'That's so sweet of you, Dick, but I'm really not ready to retire yet. I love the job. I really don't know what's the matter with me, unless that business with Dr Ransome took more out of me than I supposed at the time. And it's greedy of me to want a few days away when I've only recently had our lovely honeymoon.'

'It's not greedy at all, and we will get away soon, I promise. Unfortunately I'm going to be rather busy this next little while, trawling through bank records and the like, trying to find out where all the money has gone that Mitchell Mills stole from his clients.'

'Won't he tell you?'

'According to him it's all gone, used to pay off a gambling debt.'

'It must be a pretty big debt, then! Where has he been, Monte Carlo?'

'Something to do with organized crime here in England, I gather, and he says it's more than his life's worth for him to inform on the big boys.'

'Do you think that's true?'

Dick shrugged. 'Who knows? That's his story, and he's sticking to it. Anyway, the sooner I get started on this job, the sooner we can get away. I knew when I applied for this detective lark that it wouldn't involve regular hours, so I can't grumble if I'm tied up now.'

Maudie could see that Dick loved his work, and she was pleased for him that he'd won the chance to transfer to the detective side of the police force. And she'd spoken truly when she told him that she loved her career in midwifery. If only she could shelve this worry about the arrogant Nurse Gregg, she'd feel a whole lot better.

* * *

'Harold has agreed to play Sherlock Holmes,' Mrs Blunt said, when Maudie went to ask what was happening. 'Mind you, he thinks this is just a storm in a teacup because Nurse Gregg is such a lovely young thing. Oh, I've seen her in action! I'm not sure if she's in awe of Harold as a man of the cloth and reacting accordingly, but it's certainly butter-wouldn't-melt when she's in his presence!'

'She's probably like that with any man. That's one reason I don't want to approach Councillor Reeves on this. She'd come up smelling of roses, and I'd be written off as a sour old dame clinging to outmoded ideas.'

They were interrupted by Perkin, the vicarage cat, who strolled in, complaining loudly. He approached his mistress with determination and began to drag his claws down her skirt.

'Do stop that, Perkin,' she said. 'What's the matter with you? You've had your breakfast!' The cat continued to pester her and she stood up with a sigh. 'I'm sorry, Nurse. I'd better give him something or he'll keep this up until I do. What were you saying?'

Maudie laughed. 'Oh, nothing important! Just being catty, really. But this situation really isn't funny, you know. The National Health Service has been touted as something marvellous that will do away with all the problems of the past. Available to all, at no cost; a brave new world. You have to admit that it hasn't quite worked out that way in Llandyfan.'

The two women sat still for a while without speaking. The early-morning sunshine made patterns on the kitchen floor, reflecting the tendrils of ivy that wafted in the breeze outside the open window. The clock on the wall ticked its way through the minutes, drowned out at times by the joyful twittering of birds in the trees outside.

Looking at Mrs Blunt's pensive expression, Maudie had no doubt that her friend was remembering all the problems that had beset the health service locally. Doctors had come and gone. Maudie had soldiered on, as she had done during the war, valiantly looking after the people of the whole district and even lending a hand further afield at times. In theory, things should be easier now, with the coming of Nurse Gregg, but if anything they were worse.

'Don't forget that it's only been two years,' Mrs Blunt said slowly. 'Since the NHS started, I mean. There are bound to be bugs to iron out at first. Oh, I know it's easy for me to say; you are the one having to deal with the problems while I'm only observing from the sidelines. I wish there was something I could do to help.'

'There is!' Maudie said, her eyes dancing. 'Why can't you go and make some parish visits? Isn't that what vicars' wives are supposed to do? People are more likely to talk to a woman if they have complaints about medical treatment, or the lack of it.'

'Of course I make visits, when the need arises. But I can hardly go calling on people right after Harold has already been there.'

'I'm sure you can come up with a reason. What about some scheme to repair the church kneelers?'

'The Mothers' Union sees to all that.'

'Or a more artistic way of doing the flowers.'

'The Altar Guild.'

Maudie huffed crossly. 'Really, Mrs Blunt! Don't you want to help me?'

'I do, I do! Only I'm not some sort of Miss Marple. I don't think I'm devious enough by nature. And if Harold ever found out what I was up to, he wouldn't be at all pleased. For such a mild man, he holds strong views about the place of clergy wives in their husbands' parishes, and stirring up trouble isn't on his list of acceptable deeds.'

'Then look at it this way. Perhaps Nurse Gregg really isn't guilty of anything more than a bit of mismanagement and a sharp tongue. In that case you'll be doing her a favour if you can prove that.'

'I suppose so . . . '

'And if, on the other hand, there is trouble brewing, the sooner it can be put right, the better. Either discontent will fester until there's an uproar in the parish, or people will stop asking the girl for help — and some important symptom may be overlooked until it's too late to be dealt with.'

Perkin rattled his empty dish impatiently. Mrs Blunt stood up. 'All right!' she mumbled. 'All right!'

Maudie wasn't sure whether this was said in response to her appeal, or to the cat. She hoped it was the former.

12

'Stone the crows!'

Maudie looked up sharply in response to Dick's outburst. Postman Bert Harvey had just been with the first delivery, and one of the envelopes had presumably held startling news.

'What's the matter? It's not the electricity bill again, is it? I have no idea why it was so high last time. I'm always so careful not to leave too many lights burning.'

'No, it's not that,' Dick said. 'Come and sit down, Maudie.'

'What for? I have to get the washing-up done in a hurry. I'm running a bit late as it is, and you'll have to get off in a minute, too.'

'The crocks can wait. Listen, love. How would it strike you if we had to move away from here?'

Maudie was flabbergasted. 'Move from Llandyfan, you mean? What is it, Dick?

Are you being transferred?'

'No, no. I meant, move from this house.'

'I don't know. I've never thought about it.' She was a married woman now, and she was aware at the back of her mind that if Dick's job took him away from the area she would, of course, go with him. 'Whither thou goest, I will go.' The woman in the Bible who had said that had been speaking to her mother-in-law, but the principle was the same. Wives went where their husbands led.

'We don't have time to discuss this now,' Dick said, 'but you have to know what it's all about. It would come as too much of a shock to you if you learned of it from somebody else.'

'Dick! Don't keep me in suspense! Has somebody died?'

'This letter is from the parish council. This cottage is being put up for sale, and they are giving us the first refusal.'

Having dropped his bombshell, Dick kissed her on the cheek and left for work. Stunned, Maudie arranged her uniform cap on her newly-shorn locks, and prepared to do likewise. If the roof had fallen in, it could not have come as a greater shock.

All day long as she went about her duties, the thought of losing her home hovered at the back of her mind like a great black bird of prey. Suddenly the cottage seemed so very dear to her. She loved the little rooms with their low, dark-beamed ceilings. Every nook and cranny was so familiar to her that if she closed her eyes she could summon up every inch of the place in her thoughts. She no longer had to fumble for a light switch or a door latch; her hand was in tune with her mind and every gesture was automatic.

She remembered how indignant she had felt when Dr Donald Dean had come to the village, assuming that the cottage would be his for the taking because the council owned it, and he had been hired by them. She thought with a pang of the plans she and Dick had made for the future in that place: nothing very remarkable, just the ordinary little hopes and dreams of any married couple. She envisaged pleasant winter evenings spent in front of that fireplace, with Dick doing his football pools and herself darning his socks or listening to the wireless. Dick had plans to have a vegetable garden next year, and had already dug his patch over twice and ordered a seed catalogue. Would all that be taken away from them now? It was too cruel!

When Maudie had first come to Llandyfan before the war, one of the attractions that drew her to the place was that the cottage was tied to the job. She didn't pay rent as such, in that no landlord called on her weekly to collect her money. A sum was deducted from her salary, of course, but it was a reasonable one for the accommodation provided, and she had been delighted with the arrangement. It certainly beat living in a bedsitter, hands down.

She had experienced a few qualms when she married Dick, expecting that she would have to hand in her notice, but when she had been invited to stay on part-time those fears had been allayed. True, they had been expecting a request to pay a modest rent now that Dick was, in effect, the householder, but that would not have affected them badly. Dick had been paying for digs throughout his working life and had budgeted accordingly.

There was one bright spot on the horizon. If the house sold quickly and the Bryants had to move out, the council would have to do without Maudie's services, and that might make them think twice about going ahead with their plan to sell. It was imperative to have a midwife within cycling distance of the remote farms, and Nurse Gregg did not have the expertise to respond to women in labour. Very few of the local people possessed a car, and although there was an excellent ambulance service that could quickly transport a woman to hospital, nobody really wanted to go into hospital to have their babies.

Besides, there was much more to the midwife's craft than simply assisting at the birth. Maudie provided excellent pre- and post-natal care, a good part of which was lending a friendly presence to calm the everyday fears connected with childbirth and motherhood. Male doctors might well have superior training, but nothing could beat having another woman to confide in. No man could really understand what it was like to give birth.

★　★　★

Dick, too, had given the matter a great deal of thought during the day. When Maudie had cleared away the tea things and they were settled in their matching armchairs, he brought the subject up again.

'I think I'll go and see Reeves. Find out what they're asking for the house. The letter didn't say, but they must have something in mind.'

'Oh, Dick, we could never afford to buy a place, you know that!'

'There's no harm in asking, old girl. Besides, where are we supposed to go if they turn us out of here? It's impossible to find decent places to rent — or any sort of place at all, come to that! We can hardly pitch a tent on the common when winter comes!'

Maudie ignored that. 'Where would we ever get the money? Would the bank lend it to us?' She remembered how cheerfully they had joked about not wanting to apply to Arthur Ramsey for financial help!

'Not exactly,' Dick said. 'We'd have to get a mortgage. The big difficulty would be coming up with a suitable down-payment, unless I could get a win on the pools.'

'Fat chance! I don't know why you bother with those things, week after week. They never come up.'

'Hope springs eternal, Maudie. Never mind that. I suppose we should count our pennies and see how much we're worth, between us.'

Maudie sighed. They were both thrifty people with modest savings in the post office, and they hadn't yet spent the wedding gift they'd received from the council, but that would never be enough. And any mortgage they might receive would be based on Dick's salary alone. A woman's earnings were considered to be pin money only, liable to fade away if she became pregnant or grew tired of working outside the home.

'I think I'll pop round and see old Reeves this evening, after the chemist's shop is closed,' Dick mused.

'I'll come with you.'

'No, love, I think it best if I go on my own. Have a chat with him man-to-man,' Dick said. 'I may be able to negotiate a rent of some sort. Who knows, maybe that's what they want, some sort of income from the property.'

And, if necessary, apply a little moral blackmail, along the lines of: how could they possibly think of turning their only midwife out of her home after years of faithful service? The NHS was supposed to make health care more accessible to the ordinary citizen, not less!

* * *

Sitting in Councillor Reeves' 1930s brick villa, listening to the man pontificate, Dick realized that he didn't care for the

115

fellow very much. It wasn't just his patronizing manner, or the way he had of looking at people as if he had a bad smell under his nose, but his air of speaking as if he knew better than everybody else.

'Times are changing, Detective Sergeant. We have the National Health Service now.'

As if I didn't know, thought Dick, wriggling in his seat. There was a crack in the leather and the horsehair stuffing was prickling his thigh.

'In the past, we employed the nurses and provided living quarters for them. Our medical personnel had to collect the appropriate fees from their patients, which often proved less than satisfactory.'

Do get on with it, you old fool. I don't need a social history of rural medical care! Dick said to himself. *Steady, Bryant! Antagonizing the chap won't help! Keep calm and carry on!*

'How much were you thinking of asking for the cottage?' he said aloud.

'Possibly three thousand pounds.'

'Three thousand quid! You can't be serious! This is Llandyfan, not the

Cotswolds! It's an old country cottage where the village cooper lived back in old Queen Victoria's day. It's true it's been modernized a bit, with electricity and sanitation laid on, but it's still a very ordinary dwelling.'

Reeves smiled smugly. 'And one that many a family would give their eye teeth to possess. In fact, we could have priced it higher in view of the current housing shortage, but the rest of the committee voted in favour of a quick sale. Money is needed for drainage at Long Bottom, and the bridge below the weir is in dire need of repair. We can't afford to ignore a badly-needed source of revenue like your cottage.'

Dick swallowed hard. 'But my wife is your local midwife, man! What will happen to the local women if Maudie is forced out of the district?'

'I'm sure that Nurse Gregg is most competent to fill in where necessary, and she doesn't need to have accommodation provided for her because she stops with her aunt.'

One last throw of the dice, Dick

thought, aware that he had failed. 'And where are we supposed to go when we've been evicted? This is a fine return for my wife's years of service, I must say!'

'All good things come to an end. Nurse Bryant is a married woman now, and as such it is your duty to provide for her; not mine, or that of my colleagues. Now, I must say goodnight, Detective Sergeant. I have not yet had my evening meal and my wife will be getting anxious to serve it.'

Maudie looked up hopefully when Dick came in. 'How did it go, then?'

'It's no use, I'm afraid. We haven't a hope of meeting their price, so we'd better start looking around for somewhere to go.'

'Oh, well. At least we tried.'

'I didn't say we were giving up without a fight, Maudie. When people sell a house they always set the asking price higher than what they hope to settle for in the end. So we should make them an offer at a more realistic figure and see what happens.'

'Make them an offer? What with?'

'I'll go to a bank and see if they'll give

me a mortgage. That will be a start. Naturally, if that doesn't happen we'll be out of luck, but I don't see why they should turn me down. I have a steady job and a reliable income.'

Maudie sighed. 'Of course you must give it a go, love, and I only wish it could work, but don't count on it too much, eh? Far from accepting a lower figure, the council may find a buyer who is prepared to go even higher. People are so desperate for housing they'll go to any lengths to find a place. Somebody with private means may come along and beat us to it.'

Dick said nothing. She was probably right, and he knew that. It was just that he loved Maudie so much and he would have given her the moon, if he could. She asked so little of life. All she wanted was to remain in the little cottage that had been her home for the past few years, and he couldn't even give her that. Right now the moon seemed more accessible than his chances of owning their little love nest.

13

'I've done it! I've spoken to the aunt!'

'You've done what?!'

'I've called at the prefabs and spoken to Nurse Gregg's aunt. June Faber, her name is. The girl's father's sister.' Mrs Blunt beamed proudly.

Maudie was staggered. 'You mean you just waltzed in there and asked her what the girl gets up to when she's supposed to be seeing patients? I wonder she didn't see you off with a flea in your ear.'

The vicar's wife looked smug. 'Oh, I was far more subtle than that, Nurse Bryant! I took a few copies of the parish magazine with me, and I called at every house on Larkspur Road. That's that long section of the prefabs ending at the cricket ground. I pretended I was there as the vicar's wife, to invite people to attend St John's.'

'Sneaky!'

'No, not really. I am who I said I was,

and I'd truly like to see more people in the congregation. We would make them most welcome. Actually, though, I don't think I'm cut out to be a missionary. I racked up two Wesleyan Methodists, a Jehovah's Witness, three atheists and one 'we don't want none of that here'. By the time I reached Mrs Faber's place, I'd changed my tune and said I wanted to welcome the new nurse to the community.'

'I see. And was Nurse Gregg at home?'

'No, she was not, but I did learn something very interesting. Mrs Faber told me all about it over the tea cups.'

'And what might that be?'

'Nurse Gregg is setting her cap at Dr Dean!'

Maudie's first thought was that if that pair managed to get together then they deserved each other. She had run afoul of the arrogant Dr Dean when he had come into the area three years earlier, having bought into old Dr Mallory's practice at Midvale. Dr Mallory had since died, and Donald Dean had taken up residence in his old house there. Maudie saw little of him; as far as she was concerned, that was all to the good.

He was supposed to have a partner who would take care of the Llandyfan district, working out of the former gatehouse at the manor that had been converted into a surgery, but at present the job was vacant. Thus, Donald Dean was the doctor to whom Nurse Gregg had to report when necessary. Maudie said as much now to her friend.

Mrs Blunt shook her head. 'June Faber thinks it's more than that. One day last week, the doctor actually called at the house to pick Nurse up in his car. June was all of a twitter about it, saying how fantastic the man is, with film-star good looks.'

'Handsome is as handsome does!' Maudie grumbled, quoting her grandmother, who always distrusted a man she felt was too good-looking. 'Anyway, they were probably on their way to see a patient, somebody whom Nurse needed a second opinion on. There's no doctor at our surgery now, and not everyone can get over to Midvale to see the doctor there.'

'She wasn't wearing her uniform, then, so what do you make of that? To quote Auntie, the girl was all dressed up like a dish of fish!'

'As you say, it's very interesting,' Maudie said, 'but it doesn't mean that she's neglecting her work, which is what we want to know about. And Dr Dean may be many things, but he's a stickler for following proper medical procedure. If he thought for a moment that the patients were being neglected, he'd scorch Nurse Gregg's ears and report her to the parish medical committee like greased lightning. And probably give me a rocket too for good measure, even though I'm not responsible for the medical patients any longer.'

'Mrs Faber did let slip that she was worried about the girl having to go over to Midvale so much. After all, it's twelve miles each way on the bus, and that costs money. Nurse tells her she has to go there on medical business, but surely that can't be right? She can consult the doctor over the telephone, and one would suppose the

NHS covers the cost of official calls?'

Maudie ran her fingernails along her bottom teeth, wondering if there was any more to this than the girl running after Dr Dean — which, after all, she was free to do unless he objected to it.

'What was your overall impression, then?'

'Frankly, I wonder if the girl is so besotted with the good doctor that she's neglecting her duties in order to spend time with him. And if he feels the same about her,' Mrs Blunt went on, warming to her theme, 'he may not realize just how much time she's spending away from them. Perhaps he genuinely thinks that she has a certain amount of time on her hands because you two have more or less split up the work between you now.'

Maudie smiled. 'Thanks for trying, anyway. At least we're no worse off than before.'

'Oh, I'll be going back again,' Mrs Blunt told her. 'Mrs Faber lost her husband during the war, and if that wasn't enough she was bombed out as well. She's new to this area, having been rehoused here, and she hasn't got to know anybody yet. The poor soul is lonely and that's why she agreed to take her niece in. She begged me to come again, and I said I would.'

Maudie's conscience twinged. 'Look here, Mrs Blunt, you go and chat to the woman by all means, but don't feel that I want you to use her to keep tabs on Melanie. That would seem like a betrayal of friendship, somehow.'

Mrs Blunt's face lit up in a beautiful smile that took years off her age. 'I was hoping you'd say that, Nurse! Of course, if I hear anything about an engagement, that would be fair game!'

'You bet it would!' Maudie agreed. 'That's not gossip, that's big news!'

★   ★   ★

Dick came home looking rather pleased with himself. He had gone into the bank where he usually deposited his pay, and had been told that his application for a mortgage, should he decide to make one, would receive favourable consideration.

He was looked upon as a good risk, since he had a worthwhile career in which he was expected to go far, and in addition he was a married man.

'I don't know what that has to do with anything,' Maudie protested. 'For all they know I could spend everything you make on diamonds or mink coats.'

'Fat chance, old girl. I'm not in the diamond and mink league.'

'So I've noticed. I have to depend on the likes of John Parsons to bring me furs.'

'What's that?' Dick frowned. 'Who is John Parsons?'

Maudie laughed at the expression on her husband's face. 'It's all right; he's the gamekeeper on Cora Beasley's estate. I've brought every one of his five children into the world. That pie you had the other night came courtesy of him; well, not the actual pie. The rabbit still had its fur on when he handed it to me. That's all I meant.'

'You're a fool, Maudie Bryant,' Dick told her, 'and I love you to bits.' He picked her up and whirled her around until she screamed for mercy.

'For goodness' sake, put me down before the neighbours come running!'

'They wouldn't dare. They know we're recently married; they'd think we were having an orgy and be afraid to look.'

'That only goes to show you don't know the folk around here, Dick Bryant! They'd love to know what we get up to on the quiet. Why do you think I insisted on keeping the curtains closed when we were on honeymoon?'

'Surely not!' He frowned again, not sure whether to believe her.

She threw her head back and roared with laughter. 'I had you going for a minute there, didn't I, Dick Bryant? Call yourself a detective? If I told you the moon was made of blue cheese, I bet you'd have to stop and think about it for a minute before you ruled it out.'

'It's people like you who give the police a bad name,' Dick said, reaching for an apple from the bowl on the sideboard and biting into it. 'In future, I shan't listen to a word you say.'

14

'I think we should get a dog,' Dick mused, gazing out of the window at a woman stumbling by, towed by a frisky golden Labrador. It was a Saturday morning; the Bryants had just finished a leisurely breakfast and were now trying to decide what to do with this rare off-duty day together.

'A dog!' Maudie said. 'What made you think of that?'

Dick patted his tummy. 'If we had a dog I'd have to walk it on a regular basis, and that might deal with the unwanted side-effects of your excellent cooking.'

'It would be cheaper if you just exercised a bit of restraint,' she told him. 'Two sausages instead of four, for instance.'

'Don't be silly. I couldn't let them go to waste, could I? Waste not, want not!'

Maudie looked at him lovingly. 'So

what sort of dog did you have in mind? A sausage dog?'

'Ha ha, very funny.'

Their banter was interrupted by the shrill ringing of the telephone. 'Are you going to get that, Maudie, or shall I?' Dick muttered, reluctant to spoil the mood.

'It's probably for you. I don't have any expectant mothers coming to the boil.'

Maudie watched her husband as his expression changed from mild interest to one of grave concern.

'I see. Now, will you run through that again, Mr Bull? What exactly were you doing, and where was this? Millwood Farm, you say? Is that part of Mrs Beasley's estate?' Dick ignored his wife's nodding and the thumbs-up sign she was making.

'Yes, yes, I understand. Now please listen carefully. Leave everything exactly as it is until I get there. No, do not attempt to cover up the remains. Leave everything to me. Meanwhile, I want you to stand guard and make absolutely sure that nobody comes anywhere near the scene. Have you got that, Mr Bull? Right, then. I'll be with you as soon as I can.' Dick hung up the phone.

By now Maudie was doing her best to get in on the act, raising her eyebrows in a frantic attempt to learn what was going on. 'Not now, Maudie. I have to contact the Chief.' He picked up the earpiece again, ready to make another call.

Maudie subsided. At least Dick hadn't told her to leave the room. Something was definitely up, and she was all agog to know what it was. Moments later, she found herself fervently wishing she'd minded her own business. There wasn't much that threw Maudie Bryant off her stride, but this was just too gruesome.

'Before you ask, Maudie, you can't come with me, is that clear? Just stay in the house and I'll fill you in later. All right?' Struggling into his jacket, Dick spoke to her in an unusually stern tone of voice.

Maudie nodded. She would obediently keep away from the scene of the crime — at least, for now — but that didn't mean she had to stay indoors like an obedient little wife. She had to talk to somebody about this, and who better than her friend, Joan Blunt? Exchanging her carpet slippers for a pair of brogues, she sped round to the vicarage, almost colliding with Perkin as she rounded the corner past the lilacs. He lashed his tail and spat at her, but she barely noticed.

Mrs Blunt was in her kitchen with her arms plunged up to the elbows in a sink full of soap suds. She turned in surprise when Maudie appeared in the doorway, panting.

'Hello, Nurse! You're up and about early! Is there something wrong? You look a bit flushed.'

Maudie sat down at the table without being asked, and promptly burst into tears.

Mrs Blunt approached Maudie, wiping her hands on her apron as she came. 'Dear, dear, we can't have this! Shall I fetch the medicinal brandy, or will a strong cup of tea do the trick? I can pop the kettle on and make a fresh brew in a jiffy.'

'Don't mind me,' Maudie said, sniffing into a crumpled hankie. 'I'll be all right in a minute. Where's the vicar?'

'In his study, I think, wrestling with tomorrow's sermon. Shall I fetch him?'

'No, please don't. I just wanted to make sure he can't hear us.'

Mrs Blunt waited patiently. Many years of listening to stories involving the trials and tribulations of her husband's parishioners had taught her that it was best not to ask too many questions when someone was as distressed as Maudie seemed to be. All would be revealed in time.

At last Maudie gulped, gave one final sniff, and turned her tear-stained face to her friend.

'Dick has been called out to the manor estate, Mrs Blunt. To Millwood Farm, to be exact.'

'Oh, yes?'

'George Bull was out early this morning, ploughing Long Acre Field. To cut a long story short, he turned up a dead baby!'

'Oh, my goodness! How terrible! Did

he say what happened to the poor little thing?'

'Dick said the poor man was rather incoherent, as well he might be, but obviously it's a suspicious death, so of course DI Goodwood has been called in. Dick telephoned Midvale before he went over to see George.'

The kitchen clock ticked its way through the minutes as the two women sat, quietly contemplating the sad fact of a tiny person whose days had been cut short before it had had a chance to live. Then Maudie's face contorted and the tears began to flow again. 'And I can't help thinking it's all my fault!' she burst out.

Mrs Blunt patted her on the hand. 'Are you afraid that someone has given birth without summoning you, and that the baby was stillborn, Nurse? Are any of your patients due around this time?'

Maudie shook her head. 'It couldn't be that. Even if it was some stranger passing through — a gypsy, perhaps — why would she leave the little body in a field for poor old George to find? I'm sure that abandoning a corpse must be a criminal offence, even if the death was from natural causes.'

'I don't know what to think, Nurse, but we must leave it to the police to get to the bottom of it all. There is no need for us to get involved.'

'That's just where you're wrong, Mrs Blunt. They'll need someone to identify the body, and who will they think of first? Good old midwife Maudie, of course. And I just don't think I can face it.'

'I'm sure you'll summon up the strength to cope if that turns out to be necessary,' Mrs Blunt murmured, not quite understanding why Maudie was so dismayed by the prospect. As a nurse, she must have seen death many times, and the vicar's wife knew for a fact that part of her duties here in Llandyfan had been to lay out the deceased when the need arose. And of course she had seen unnatural death before, beginning with the poor man who had been murdered near Oliver Bassett's farm!

Maudie sat hunched over at the table, holding her hands up to her face. 'I'm dreadfully afraid it's little Peggy Ann,' she whispered.

'What? You mean Peggy Ann Ramsey? No, no, it couldn't possibly be!' Mrs Blunt was appalled at the implication. 'She's in Cornwall with her granny.'

'Sheila could have come back. That husband of hers didn't want her to leave in the first place, and he may have insisted she come home. Then it all got to be too much for the poor soul and she snapped. Perhaps she shook the baby when it wouldn't stop crying. That could easily have happened.' Maudie's voice rose to a wail.

Mrs Blunt stood up. 'I'm going to fetch that brandy, and you are going to take a good swig, Nurse Bryant! And I think I'd better have a tot as well.'

'It isn't in the study, is it? I don't want the vicar to know what we're talking about.'

'No, no. I keep it hidden in the cupboard under the stairs, actually.'

'So Perkin can't get at it?' Maudie said,

in a weak attempt at levity. 'A woozy cat is all we need!' She realized that she was dangerously close to hysteria.

15

Much later, Joan Blunt opened the door to an anxious Dick Bryant. His hair was tousled and his good trousers were covered with mud. 'Have you seen my wife, Mrs Blunt? I can't find her anywhere and the breakfast dishes are still on the table. I thought she might have left me a note if she'd been called out to a patient, but I can't seem to find one anywhere.'

'Your wife is quite safe, Mr Bryant. She's upstairs, lying down.'

'She's not ill, is she?'

'No, no. Just a bit wobbly. She was rather upset about George Bull's unpleasant discovery, blaming herself, and I'm afraid I dosed her with brandy. In fact, I had a little nip myself, and I'm still a bit shaky.'

'Why on earth would she blame herself? This is nothing to do with Maudie.'

'She feels that it is very much to do with her. Look, Mr Bryant, you'd better come upstairs and talk to her. I'll show you the way.'

They found Maudie stretched out on top of the eiderdown in the spare bedroom, staring into space. When she saw her husband she burst into tears, struggling to sit up.

'Oh, Dick!' He gathered her into his arms and held her close, rocking her back and forth on the side of the bed.

'I'll just go and, er . . . ' Mrs Blunt murmured.

'No, no, you stay, Mrs Blunt. You'd better hear this. It will be all over the village by now in any case.' Dick smiled at her reassuringly, and she lowered herself into a Lloyd Loom chair and waited expectantly for what he had to say.

'Now then, my love, what's all this I hear about you blaming yourself for this child's death?'

'I should have known, Dick!'

'What should you have known?'

'Why, that poor Sheila Ramsey was more seriously depressed that anyone

138

thought. I thought I was so clever, trying to show I was on her side against that bully of a husband. I thought the baby would be safe in Cornwall with the grandmother there. It never occurred to me that they wouldn't stay there.'

'Even if they had returned, that would hardly be your fault, old girl.'

'But I should have known! Sheila Ramsey is my patient. If I'd been doing my job properly I'd have made sure that she was still away. And I've been running around accusing Nurse Gregg of falling down on the job when I'm guilty of negligence myself. How can I ever forgive myself, Dick?'

'What a lot of hogwash!' he told her. 'If you choose to wallow in self-pity, that's up to you, but you should wait to hear the facts before you jump to mistaken conclusions.'

'What do you mean?'

'The remains that George Bull turned up with his plough have been in the earth for a very long time, possibly a hundred years or more.'

'But I didn't hear you mention

anything like that when you rang DI Goodwood.'

'That's because I didn't know about it then. Poor Bull was so upset by what he'd found that he hardly knew what he was saying. In fact, it didn't even occur to him to call 999. He knew that you were married to a copper, so his first thought was to ring our number. All he wanted was to hand over the problem to someone else as soon as possible.'

'A hundred years!' Maudie said. 'How can you tell?'

'I can't, exactly, but it seems likely. The baby was buried in a little coffin which had come apart, either from the length of time it had been in the ground or as a result of being disturbed by the plough. The little bones were dressed in what is left of some very old-fashioned clothing; very good quality, I should say. This was no unwanted child, abandoned in haste.'

'I'm glad of that,' Mrs Blunt said softly. 'But why bury it in a field when our graveyard is so close by?'

'We may never know the answer to that,' Dick said. 'There will have to be an investigation, of course, but it may never get us anywhere after so much time has elapsed. Meanwhile, I think I should take my wife home with me. If you intend to lie about all day, Maudie Bryant, you may as well do it in your own bed!'

*   *   *

Maudie felt as if a terrible weight had rolled off her mind. What a fool she had been to suspect poor Sheila Ramsey of doing away with her lovely little girl! Still, there was something she felt bound to do before she could put the matter to rest. She still had Mrs Beadle's phone number in Cornwall, so she placed a call to that lady while Dick was luxuriating in the bath.

'How nice of you to call, Nurse!'

'I just thought I'd see how my patients are doing. Are they enjoying Cornwall?'

'Oh, yes. Sheila is feeling much more relaxed now, and little Peggy Ann has actually started sleeping through the night! Such a relief for all concerned. Between you and me, I think she was aware of the tension in that house, and reacted accordingly. Arthur is a decent man really, and a good provider, but he does tend to have some old-fashioned ideas.'

'A lot of men do.'

'I expect you see a lot of that in your practice, don't you, Nurse?'

'Sometimes. Well, I mustn't keep you, but would you mind letting me know when Sheila and the baby decide to return home? I'll want to resume my regular schedule of visits, you see.'

'Of course. And thank you so much for calling.'

Relieved, Maudie replaced the earpiece on its hook. Now she could relax. What a fool she had been to let herself get so rattled for no good reason! And it was wrong of her to have suspected poor Sheila Ramsey, even for a moment. Post-natal depression could happen to anyone, and even in very serious cases it did not automatically mean that sufferers were likely to harm their children. Yet Maudie also knew that anyone, man or woman, could snap when placed under unbearable stress, so perhaps she should not be too hard on herself.

This experience had taught her a lesson, though. She must be more forbearing when it came to Nurse Gregg. Who knew what stress the girl might be under? According to Mrs Blunt, who had heard about it from the girl's aunt, this was Melanie's first post outside a hospital setting. She might well be overwhelmed by the heavy responsibility.

★ ★ ★

Being on the spot, Dick was assigned to investigate the death of the unknown baby. As he said to Maudie, there wasn't a lot he could do about it when it appeared to have happened so long ago, a fact that was confirmed by the police surgeon. Naturally, he went around asking questions, but that had led to nothing.

'Oh, people are more than willing to speculate, but so far I've heard nothing that makes sense. The most reasonable suggestion so far is that somebody from far away was visiting Llandyfan when she gave birth, or passing through, and the baby was stillborn, or died soon afterwards.'

'Which happened a lot more frequently a century ago than it does now,' Maudie agreed.

'And because the mother lived so far away, she was unable to take the baby back with her for burial. She could hardly spend days in a coach with a dead infant on her lap.'

'That's all very well, Dick, but it still doesn't explain what the baby was doing in George Bull's field. Why didn't the vicar of the day insist on giving it a Christian burial here at St. John's?'

'And come to that,' Dick mused, 'how is it that the coffin hasn't come to light before now? This is a real puzzler, Maudie.'

★ ★ ★

Two days later Dick had another case to pursue. 'I've been called over to Baldene,' he told Maudie. 'I don't know when I'll be back, so don't wait tea for me.'

144

'I don't think I've ever been there,' she said. She knew where it was on the map, of course — a few miles past Midvale — but she'd never had occasion to go there as it was well out of her territory.

'As far as I'm aware, it's usually a pretty law-abiding place, but now they've had a suspicious death in the cinema.'

'I take it you mean in real life, and not in a Hollywood movie?'

'Of course. Some poor chap has been found dead, sitting upright in his seat in the one-and-nines. An usherette noticed him when she was going off duty. She shone her torch on him and called out to him, but when he didn't answer she assumed he'd gone to sleep. When she went up to him and tapped him on the shoulder, he toppled over and landed in a heap at her feet.'

'Poor girl. She must have got a nasty shock.'

'I daresay. So that's the story, and I've been taken off the baby case here. The Chief reckons we'll never get to the bottom of it, and we don't have the manpower to devote to it any longer.'

'Oh!' Maudie said.

Dick regarded her quizzically. 'I can guess what you're thinking, Maudie Bryant!'

'Me? I'm not thinking anything,' she told him, trying to look innocent.

'Don't come that with me; I know you too well. You're thinking this is a nice little mystery for you to get your teeth into, aren't you?'

'It's only because there's a baby involved,' she pleaded. 'And no harm can come to me if I do, because even if the child died as a result of foul play, the people involved have been dead for donkey's years.'

'I suppose it can't do any harm if you poke about a bit. It's not as if you'd be interfering in a police investigation. Just make sure you don't spend so much time on it that you neglect your long-suffering husband, that's all! I still expect my meals on the table and my shirts washed and ironed, is that clear?'

'Oh, don't be such an idiot!' she said, taking a swing at him.

He took her into his arms and planted

a kiss on her laughing mouth. 'I love you, Maudie Bryant!'

'I love you too, Dick Bryant! Now get going, or you'll be late, and your boss will blame it on me.'

'As well he might, you temptress,' Dick said, snatching up his trilby and running out to the car.

16

Maudie made her way to the village shop, not quite knowing what she was going there to buy. It was difficult to know what to plan for their tea. Dick might be delayed over at Baldene, in which case she'd be eating alone and wouldn't need an elaborate meal, or he could arrive on time, expecting more than simply a boiled egg and soldiers.

Once there she picked up a tin of corned beef, deliberating with it in her hand. She could heat it up in the frying pan to serve with mashed potato and some sort of vegetable, or it would do equally well in a sandwich with chutney if he walked in late, feeling peckish. She pulled a face, remembering hospital meals where corned beef was served to the accompaniment of beetroot and lumpy potatoes. She had disliked said combination intensely, especially whilst she was on night duty, when meals were

148

eaten topsy-turvy. It was bad enough eating dinner at eight o'clock in the morning without having to face horrible mixtures like that! Still, Dick liked corned beef, so why should he be denied it simply because of her prejudices? There was nothing to stop her having an egg if he failed to put in an appearance.

'Are you going to the funeral, Nurse?' Mrs Hatch took Maudie's money and rang it up into the till.

'Funeral?' Maudie's mind was still on her plans for her husband's evening meal. 'Who died? I must have missed something.'

'Perhaps 'funeral' isn't the right word under the circumstances. I meant the vicar laying that murdered baby to rest. I heard they're not having a service in the church, just a committal in the graveyard. After all, we don't know who the kiddy was, so who's to say it was even Church of England? Could have been anything.'

'The police have found no evidence that the baby was murdered, Mrs Hatch. I repeat, no evidence at all. According to the police surgeon, it probably died a very long time ago, and in the old days child mortality was much higher than it is today. A great many children died in infancy in our grandparents' time.'

'Oh, I know that, Nurse. But if this one died of natural causes, how come it was buried in that field instead of consecrated ground?'

Maudie shook her head. 'Your guess is as good as mine.'

'And it seems funny to me that it's never come to light before now. It's not as if that field's been left lying fallow for a hundred years or more. George Bull's a good farmer, keeping to the four-fold rotation of crops, same as they taught us in school.'

'Oh, I know the answer to that,' Maudie told her. 'Mr Bull decided to cut back a lot of gorse that had grown up on the edge of that field, to reclaim a bit more land. He should have got to it sooner, he told Dick, but with most of the able-bodied men having gone away to the war, including his own sons, he's been so short-handed he's never got around to it until now.'

'Should have put them land girls on the job, then.'

'I daresay they had enough to do without that. Well, to answer your first question, Mrs Hatch, I expect I shall go to the burial.'

'I thought you would, you being a midwife,' the shopkeeper said, although Maudie couldn't quite follow her line of reasoning. 'I thought I'd shut up the shop that day, out of respect, like.' If Maudie thought this was going too far, she felt it wise to say nothing. Thanking the older woman, she popped the tin of beef into her string bag and set out for home.

★   ★   ★

Fortunately, the day of the burial was fine, with only a stiff breeze to whip some fleecy white clouds across the deep blue sky. It appeared that Llandyfan had taken the unknown baby to its collective heart. Carpenter Ben Giles had produced a beautiful little white coffin to replace the shattered box found in the original grave, and the Mothers' Union had held an ad

151

hoc meeting in which they had voted to dip into their funds to provide a suitable grave marker. There was some disagreement as to the wording on this as they had no name for the baby and not even a year of death.

One member suggested 'Known Unto God' as a suitable inscription, but this was rejected by another woman who said it had been used on the crosses in the battlefields of Flanders, and was therefore inappropriate, possibly even irreverent, here. Someone else had recommended inscribing a rather sickly-sweet Victorian mourning verse found in an old scrapbook, but that idea had also been shot down on the grounds of needless expense.

All this Maudie had gleaned from the vicar's wife and passed on to Dick, who found it interesting but not particularly useful. Now she stood on the edge of the gravesite, watching the little knot of women who stood reverently waiting for the vicar to speak. Why had they come? Perhaps some were there because they were mothers who would not care to think of their own children going unattended to the grave if, heaven forbid, they were to die in distressing circumstances.

One or two might have come with the vague idea of participating in an historic event. In years to come, they would be able to say to a grandchild, 'I was there when they reburied the murdered baby, you know. That was a mystery that was never solved.'

And then there were those who had come just to see what was going on, like onlookers drawn to the scene of a road accident. And as for Maudie herself, what was she doing here? If asked to explain her motives she might have been hard-pressed to come up with a satisfactory answer, except that it was a baby, and she was a midwife, and so to some extent she could not fail to be emotionally involved.

All in all, the Reverend Harold Blunt did a satisfactory job of committing the little bones to the earth without any undue mawkish sentiment, or indeed any supposition concerning the circumstances of the original burial, which would not have been fitting.

'Our Saviour Christ said: 'Suffer little children to come unto me, and forbid them not: for of such is the kingdom of God.'' The familiar ritual continued: 'Earth to earth, ashes to ashes, dust to dust; in sure and certain hope of the Resurrection to eternal life . . . '

'Amen,' Maudie murmured with the rest of those present, believing that the little soul would have arrived in heaven long since, and so the burial today was simply the closing of a final chapter.

Unaccountably, tears came to her eyes as she joined in the singing of an old hymn familiar to her from Sunday School: *There's a home for little children, above the bright blue sky* . . . Judging by the expression of surprise on the vicar's face, this had not been part of his plan but a spontaneous move on the part of one or more of the Mothers' Union ladies. He stood patiently by until the final amen, with the wind blowing his surplice around his legs, displaying an expanse of black trouser leg.

Dick arrived home on time, sniffing the air like a Bisto Kid. 'What's for tea?' he asked, coming into the kitchen with a look of expectancy on his face.

'Cauliflower cheese and corned beef, if you'll open this blessed tin for me,' Maudie muttered. 'The key broke off the tab and now I can't get it to move.'

'Just pass me the proper tin-opener and I'll see what I can do.'

Maudie had returned from the grave-yard craving comfort food, and she had suddenly fancied cauliflower *au gratin*, luckily having the ingredients on hand. The addition of corned beef was simply an extra treat for Dick.

'I didn't expect you yet. What happened to the case you were working on?'

'Oh, it seems as if there's no reason to suspect foul play after all. We have to wait for the results of the autopsy, but it looks as if the chap probably died of natural causes: a stroke, say, or a heart attack.'

'Surely the people sitting in his row would have noticed something?'

'According to the manager there weren't a lot of people there. For all anyone knew he could have dozed off, or even have decided to sit the big picture round again, if he'd come in during the middle of the earlier showing.'

'I suppose so.'

'Our only problem is that we have no idea who the chap is. He didn't have any identification on him.'

'No wallet?'

'No. Just his ticket stub, a Yale key and some loose change. He was wearing a very good watch, though, so it doesn't look as if he was robbed. Unfortunately, we therefore can't notify his next of kin, or contact his own family doctor to see if he had any health problems. It looks as if we'll have to wait until somebody reports him missing.'

'Which may not happen if he's a bachelor,' Maudie mused. 'And if he has his own door key, that could mean a flat of his own with nobody around to notice his comings and goings.'

'My goodness; my wife, the great detective!'

'You watch your cheek, Dick Bryant! Do you want chutney or pickled red cabbage with that horrible beef?'

'Let's go mad and have both,' he replied, swinging her round and planting a sloppy kiss on the back of her neck.

17

Maudie was reluctantly vacuuming the stairs when the doorbell rang. Muttering, she turned off the Hoover and went to see who wanted her. She found a tall young man waiting on the step, quite good-looking, with black curly hair and dark eyes.

'Are you the midwife?'

'Yes, that's right.'

'Then can you come, please? The wife's in labour. Mum says to tell you there's no mad rush, but Mae should be looked at soon.'

'Yes, of course. Who is your wife, please? I mean, has she been coming to me for ante-natal care?'

'Her name is Mae Green, and I'm Brian. We've been living in Gloucester until recently, but then I lost my job, so we had to come home to Mum. We live out on the Brookfield road.'

'And has your wife seen her doctor

there? She's been getting regular check-ups?'

Brian Green grimaced. 'No, she hasn't. She doesn't like doctors much, and us Greens are a healthy lot.'

Maudie sighed inwardly. She could only hope that the fellow was right in his assumptions. Meanwhile, the sooner she saw her patient, the better. 'If you'll hang on five minutes, I'll come back with you now. I'll have to get my uniform on and leave a note for my hubby, just in case I'm not back before he comes home.'

'Right you are!' Giving her a small salute, he ambled out to the gate where his bicycle lay waiting on the grass.

Maudie bundled the Hoover into the cupboard under the stairs before racing up to her bedroom to scramble into her uniform dress. There was no time to waste. For all the young father's laid-back attitude, there was no telling what stage of labour his young wife had reached — although presumably his mother had some idea, having given birth herself.

They had two miles to go, cycling into a stiff wind, and Maudie was thankful

159

when the young man indicated that his family home lay just ahead. It was a small stone house, smaller than Maudie's cottage, and from the number of windows she assumed it was a typical two-up, two-down farm labourer's residence. Brian had explained that there were eight of them living under the one roof just now: his parents, his three younger brothers, his elderly grandmother, and now the two of them. Maudie couldn't imagine where they all slept, although she was well aware that, years ago, people had often brought up large families in such dwellings.

Brian's mother came to the door to greet them, wiping her hands on her apron as she came.

'Hello, Nurse! I'm glad the boy managed to find you. I'm his mum, Phyllis Green.'

'How do you do! I'm Nurse Bryant.'

'Yes, we've heard of you from the landlord of the Royal Oak.'

'That sounds as if I'm an old soak!' Maudie quipped.

'Oh, no, he had nothing but good

things to say about you. I'm told you're something of a sleuth. I envy you. I'm an Agatha Christie fan myself.'

Maudie laughed. 'Well, I'm wearing my midwife's cap today! May I see my patient now?'

She examined young Mrs Green and ascertained that all was well. 'Things are chugging along nicely, but you'll be a while yet,' she told her.

'You will stay with me, won't you, Nurse?' the young woman pleaded. 'I'm a bit scared, see. This being my first, I don't know what to expect.'

'I won't go anywhere,' Maudie reassured her, 'and there's no need to be frightened. Would you like me to explain to you what's going to happen?'

Mae nodded nervously. Maudie occasionally met patients who had no idea how the baby would make its appearance, and she always described the process quite early on in their appointment schedule, handing out literature on the subject as well. This girl hadn't even seen a doctor, so she might be completely in the dark. Of course, Phyllis had been through it all several times and presumably the girl had a mother of her own, but that didn't mean that these women could pass on medical knowledge in the most efficient way.

During the hours that followed, Maudie sat with Phyllis Green while Mae played cards with her husband. Phyllis seemed eager to chat, which certainly helped to pass the time, but they were interrupted several times by thumps on the ceiling and distant cries of rage.

'That's Ma off again,' Phyllis said, looking glum. 'Run up and see what she wants, will you, Brian? If it's her chamber pot she wants emptying, you'll have to do it. I'm fair worn out running up and down after her all day.'

'Can I help?' Maudie asked. 'I can go up if you like.'

'No, no; she's all right. She just gets a bit stroppy up there on her own.'

'Can't she come down here and sit with us?'

'Of course she could, but she won't. It drives her barmy when we're all crammed in here together and she says

162

she doesn't have the space to breathe. Of course she's right, really. We could just about manage until Brian and Mae turned up, but now it's a real squash. Oh, don't misunderstand me, Nurse; of course I'm glad to see them, and we had to take them in, didn't we? You have to look after your own. After Brian lost his job they couldn't pay the rent and the landlord put them out. The thing is, I just don't know what we're going to do when the baby comes.'

'Where do you all sleep at the moment?' Maudie wondered.

'Well, there's two bedrooms upstairs. My mother-in-law has one, and our three younger sons share the other, sleeping nose-to-toe in the one bed. Josh and I have the wall bed, there behind you; and as you've seen, Brian and Mae have that mattress on the floor over there. We rig up a curtain at night for a bit of privacy, though that won't help much when there's a crying baby in the house.'

Maudie looked on with fascination as Phyllis demonstrated how her bed could be pulled out when it was needed and folded up into the wall again, creating space for daytime use. She had heard of these beds but had never actually seen one before.

Brian clattered his way down the stairs, looking annoyed. 'She wants a cup of tea, Mum. And she wants her bed straightening and she won't let me do it. Says you've got nothing to do down here and it's about time you showed her some respect.'

'Oh, put the kettle on,' his mother said wearily.

'Why don't you let me go and see to her?' Maudie suggested. 'Tell me something about her; her general condition, and so on.'

'Not much to tell. She's Josh's old mum, she's eighty-nine. She's crippled with arthritis and crabby with it. I feel sorry for the poor old girl; getting on in years is no joke, but she can be a trial at times, and that's a fact.'

'We should be able to manage something to lighten the load for you, Mrs Green. I'll be looking in on Mae and the baby for a while and I can help with your mother-in-law then. After that, Nurse Gregg can take over. She's the new young nurse for Llandyfan and district.'

'That should give us some relief,' Phyllis agreed.

★ ★ ★

'Who might you be?' the old lady demanded. 'Who do you think you are, coming into my room like this? I sent for Phyllis, not you!'

'I'm Nurse Bryant, the midwife. I'm here to deliver Mae's baby.'

'Mae? I don't know any Mae!'

'Your grandson's wife.'

'Stuff and nonsense. My grandson don't have a wife. Just childer, all of them are.'

Maudie surmised that Mrs Green was suffering to some extent from senility, and that was adding to the difficulty between the generations in the home. She swiftly tidied the bed, fluffed up the pillows, and handed the old woman the cup of tea she'd carried upstairs.

'Shall I sit here?' Without waiting for an

165

answer she sat down on the bedside chair, first moving aside a pile of clean sheets. The room was tidy, if sparsely furnished, and it was evident that old Mrs Green was well cared for, even if her daughter-in-law was living under stress.

'Have you lived here long, Mrs Green?' she began.

'Course I have. I come here as a bride, didn't I, back in 1879.'

'My goodness, that's a long time ago!'

'I'm eighty-nine,' the old lady said proudly. 'If I live to see next Michaelmas I'll be ninety then.'

'You'll live to be a hundred,' Maudie assured her.

'Not sure I want to, with all the goings-on in the world today. We've just had a war, you know.'

'Yes, I know all about it.'

'My boy was in it, and lived to tell the tale. Oh, not our Joshua, him as lives here with me. It's Albert I'm talking about, his older brother. They've given him a medal, you know, with bars on it to show where he's been fighting. Johannesburg, Pretoria, Driefontein. A lot of funny foreign names like that.'

'Oh, yes.' Maudie realized that Mrs Green was remembering the Boer War, which had been over for fifty years. Her brain had blanked out the memory of the two world wars they'd had since then. Her condition was typical of many older people who seemed caught in limbo between the past and the present.

'Well, I'm glad to have met you, Mrs Green,' she said, standing up to leave. 'I must go down and see how young Mrs Green is getting along. Just think, in a few hours from now you'll be a great-grandmother. Won't that be lovely?'

'Don't know what you mean!'

'Brian's wife is about to have a baby, Mrs Green.'

'Poor baby. They found his bones after all,' the old lady said.

A shrill cry sounded from down below, and Maudie scuttled downstairs as fast as she could. Young Mae's face was flushed with distress, but Maudie was able to reassure her at once.

'It's all right, Mae. Your waters have broken, and that's a good sign.'

'But I've wet myself. I'm so embarrassed!'

'You don't have to be. This simply means that the fluid-filled sac that encloses your baby has broken, which is what is supposed to happen. That's why I put the rubber sheet under you when I first arrived. We'll shoo your hubby out of the room while I mop you up. And while you're about it, Mr Green, I suggest you hop over to the Royal Oak, and stay there until you're sent for!'

18

Another Saturday rolled around, giving Maudie and Dick time to catch up on the events in their professional lives.

'What happened about that poor man in the cinema?' Maudie wondered.

'Oh, it seems he died of a massive stroke, so there was nothing for us to investigate after all.'

'But who was he? I thought you said nobody had come forward to report him missing?'

'Actually, his wife did come forward in the end, poor soul. She'd been away for a week visiting her mother in Kent, and as they are not on the phone the couple hadn't been in touch while she was gone. When she did get back, she was alarmed to find all the post sitting on the doormat, including a picture postcard of Canterbury Cathedral she'd sent her husband. She went to the police station in fear and trembling; and, sadly, they were able to confirm her suspicions. They took her to the mortuary and she identified the body as her husband, William Ryan.'

'Oh, dear. Well, at least it wasn't murder. She won't have that to come to terms with.'

'Are there any more biscuits?' Dick got up and rattled the tin.

'No more chocolate bikkies,' Maudie told him. 'You've just eaten the last three. I think there's some Marie or Nice in the biscuit barrel if you're that desperate.'

'No, thanks. I'm in the mood for chocolate. Don't we even have a Kit Kat in the house?'

'There was one, but I've had it.'

'Meanie!'

'Better 'meanie' than 'fatty',' Maudie said sternly. 'Unless you get that dog you're always talking about and start going for long walks, you'll really have to think about cutting back on the calories. If you don't watch out, your trousers won't fit, and that suit was too expensive to discard yet awhile.'

'Speak for yourself!' Dick said, in mock annoyance.

'I happen to have lost five pounds recently,' she said smugly.

Dick shook his head sadly. He knew when he was beaten. 'How did things turn out for that new mother of yours?'

'Young Mrs Green? Oh, very well. They have a lovely little girl, six pounds twelve ounces. The grandparents are delighted because they've only had boys in the family until now, so a granddaughter is a treat. Even the young uncles are besotted. The only person who isn't thrilled is the old granny. She seems to spend half the time thumping on the floor with her stick, which they can do without.'

* * *

Just how much stress it was really causing was made apparent to Maudie when she made her next visit to the Green's cottage. Phyllis Green met her at the door, brandishing a wooden spoon.

'You don't mean to lambaste me with that weapon, I hope?' Maudie quipped. The woman stared at it as if she wondered where it had come from.

'Oh, sorry, Nurse! I was just stirring the soup with this when I heard you knock. Honestly, I don't know what I'm doing half the time. I don't know if I'm coming or going!'

'Sit yourself down and tell me all about it, Mrs Green. And, if you don't object to my telling you what to do in your own kitchen, I believe a cup of tea is in order.'

'I don't have time! I've the rest of the washing to peg out and the dinner to see to, and a stack of mending and darning for the boys that you wouldn't believe!'

'And all of that will still be waiting when you've had a break. Don't worry about the washing, I can peg that out for you; and as for the mending, that will wait for another day. You can always teach those great big lads of yours to darn their own socks.'

'I can't afford to let things slide,' the woman wailed, 'I'm all behind like the old cow's tail.' But when Maudie continued to insist, she made the tea and brought it to the table.

'Now then,' Maudie said, 'you just tell me what all this is about.' She already knew, of course, but she wanted Phyllis Green to experience the release of getting her concerns off her chest. Sharing one's woes was half the battle in managing to cope.

'It's everything, really,' the woman sighed. 'Too much work and not enough time to do it in. Never a minute's peace with her upstairs, and now with the baby and all, it's ten times worse. Oh, little Lucy Mae is a darling and good as gold, but of course babies do cry, and that's only to be expected. When she wakes up for the two o'clock feeding the whole house is in an uproar, with Grandma thumping on the ceiling, and my hubby asking how he's supposed to get up at five if he hasn't had a decent kip.'

'I'm sure it must be difficult.'

'Difficult! You don't know the half of it, Nurse. If only we had a bedroom to spare for Brian and them, it would be a help — we could cut the noise off to some extent — but there's no hope of that as long as old Fan is alive.'

'Have you thought of putting her on the waiting list for a place in a retirement home?' Maudie ventured. It seemed to her like an ideal solution. 'She'd get the care she needs, and she might even be happier with people of her own age to talk to. Some of these places are very good, with entertainments and outings for the residents.'

'What! Put her in an old folks' home? She's always dreaded that, Nurse. People of that generation still think of it as the workhouse, you know. Something to be avoided at all costs.'

'All the same, the day may come when you don't have any other choice,' Maudie said. 'I've noticed that she is becoming quite confused. That could worsen, you know, to the point where she wanders off, or accidentally sets fire to the place because she thinks she's meant to be doing the cooking.'

'I know what you're saying,' Phyllis muttered, rocking herself back and forth on her chair, 'but it won't do. This is her house, Nurse. We promised her, you see, years ago, that if she let us come to live here, we'd always care for her, never let her be put away.'

'You mean she owns this cottage?' Maudie asked, startled.

'No, no, of course she doesn't. The likes of us don't own property! But my late father-in-law worked on the estate, you see, and this place went with the job for a married man. He brought Fanny here in 1879 and she's been here ever since. Well, my Josh is a labouring chap too, like his father before him, so he sort of inherited the place from him. But the old man was still alive when we got married, and it was his idea that Josh should bring me here to live in return for looking after the old folks in due course.'

Maudie knew that this sort of arrangement had been common years ago, when families were responsible for parents in their old age. Elderly folk who did not have grown children to look after them were indeed in danger of ending up in the dreaded workhouse.

'I do understand,' Maudie said. 'But things are different now, Mrs Green, with the new National Health Service. Your mother-in-law can be looked after in decent surroundings at no cost to you.

And she doesn't have to be abandoned! The family can visit her on a regular basis. Now, look, you don't have to come to a decision right away. What I'm suggesting is that you speak to Dr Dean, who will come and assess Mrs Green's state of health, and then we put her name on a waiting list for a suitable place. Nothing is likely to happen for a while, but when an opening does come up, you can decide then what is best to do. And by then you may find that her condition has deteriorated to the point where you can't possibly cope without professional help.'

Young Mrs Green came into the kitchen just then, cradling her baby, and the subject was dropped. 'I've had such a lovely stroll, and I'm sure Lucy Mae enjoyed it too!'

'I'm glad to hear it,' Maudie told her, smiling. 'Now then, I'm just about to put the washing out on the line; you'll come and give me a hand, won't you? I know that Grandma would love to sit with little Lucy on her lap for a few minutes.'

Surprised, Mae obediently followed her

outside, removing the clothes prop to lower the line as she came.

'I just needed a word with you in private,' Maudie said in a low voice. 'Poor Mrs Green is under tremendous pressure at the moment, and I thought that if you knew about it you might be able to help.'

'Of course, Nurse. What could I do?'

'I know you need time to recover from giving birth, but perhaps you could tackle a few small jobs, sitting down? Peeling the spuds, for instance, or darning the boys' socks.'

'Yes, I can do that. I should have thought, really. She's been so kind, taking us in when we had nowhere else to go. I know Brian feels so guilty at not being able to support me and the baby.'

'I'm sure he'll find something soon. Meanwhile, perhaps he can do something to help his mother, too. Spending time with the old lady, for instance. When she feels lonely and neglected, she takes it out on her daughter-in-law. It's all due to old age, really, and there's not much that can be done about that, except show some patience with her.'

'I can ask him,' Mae said doubtfully, 'but I don't know what he'll say. He's a bit frightened of her, I think. Last night his mum sent him up with his gran's supper on a tray, and the baby happened to be crying at the time. When Brian got up there she started shouting, saying really weird stuff. 'Don't you let that baby die, or Vicar won't bury it.' Over and over, talking like that. Brian didn't want to hear any horrible talk about our Lucy Mae dying.'

'Oh, I expect she's heard something about that little skeleton that Farmer Bull turned up with his plough,' Maudie explained. 'And she needn't worry: Mr Blunt did a lovely job of conducting the service when they reburied the child in the graveyard.'

But while Maudie was pedalling her way back to the village, the old lady's words, as recounted by Mae Green, came back to her rather forcibly.

'I wonder,' she said aloud. 'I wonder!'

19

' 'Don't let the baby die, or Vicar won't bury it', ' Mrs Blunt murmured, echoing Maudie's words. 'I don't know if you should read anything into that, Nurse. You said yourself that the old lady is wandering in her wits. Let's face it, she is getting on a bit.'

'But she might know something, don't you think?'

'Or she might not. Everyone in the district is gossiping about George Bull's find, and there was even a piece in *The Midvale Chronicle* about the burial service Harold held. Mrs Green may have overheard people talking about that, or even read the newspaper for herself.'

'She did warn young Brian not to let his baby die!'

'Probably with good reason. In her young day, children died in infancy all the time. You can't expect her to understand that life is different now.'

'But why say that Mr Blunt wouldn't bury the child if it died? It's quite obvious that he would, after he's just had a committal service for the mystery baby.'

'I really have no idea, Nurse. At this moment I'm more concerned with the living. We are desperately short of teachers for the Sunday School, and we're about to lose another one when Miss Allison retires and goes to live with her sister in Devon. I don't suppose you or Sergeant Bryant . . . '

'Oh, no,' Maudie said hastily. 'We couldn't possibly! It's our jobs, you see. We might get called away at any moment: me to a confinement, and Dick to goodness knows what. We'd hate to leave you in the lurch. That's why I've always said no to helping with the Guides, other than stepping in occasionally to test them for their first aid or home nursing badges. No, I'm afraid that a regular commitment is out.'

'I just thought I'd ask,' Mrs Blunt murmured.

'I'll keep it in mind, though. I say!

What about Nurse Gregg's Auntie June? You told me she's lonely. This could be just what she needs.'

'I don't know if she's Church of England.'

'There's only one way to find out! And as for me, I intend to go back to Fanny Green to ask her a few questions. She told me she was married in 1879. Presumably her children were born in the 1880s, even the 1890s. I wonder if our baby's bones date from that time?'

'You're surely not suggesting that Mrs Green is the mother of that child? If her baby died, why on earth would she bury it in unhallowed ground? Surely that was a crime?'

'Who knows why people do what they do?'

'Surely everyone would have known about it? There would have been questions asked. Why wasn't there a proper funeral? If the child wasn't in the family burial plot, where was it? No, Nurse, you've got it wrong, I know.'

'It may have been someone she knew,'

Maudie said stubbornly. 'Anyway, it's the only clue I've got, so I may as well keep going down that road.'

* * *

'Is Joshua Green your only child?' Maudie asked. It was as good a place to start as any. She had the old lady sitting out on the chair while she changed her sheets in readiness for the weekly wash. People approaching senility might have little awareness of what is happening in the present, but they often had total recall of the past. Mrs Green was no exception to the rule.

'Bless you, no! Seven, I've had, and lost three.'

'Three of your children have died?'

'No, no. Miscarriages, like.'

'Ah. And where are the seven now?'

'Young Josh is my baby, him that lives in this house with me.'

Maudie had to smile. 'Young Josh' was all of sixty, maybe more. 'And the others?'

'Betty lives in Midvale. Albert and

Thomas went to Australia and we never hear from them now. At first they used to send a bit of money home, but that stopped long ago. They've forgotten their poor old mum, I think. Fred died two years ago, and Martin died at Ypres. That was in the Great War.'

'I see.' Counting up mentally, Maudie realized here was one baby unaccounted for. 'That's only six, Mrs Green.'

'Is it? Oh, I forgot about Alice. She was Fred's twin. Sickly, she was. Only lived a few hours and then she died.'

This sounded promising, but Maudie could hardly come right out and ask where little Alice was buried! Instead, she smoothed down the bottom sheet with its neatly-made hospital corners, and invited Mrs Green to return to bed.

'I think I'll sit up for a while, Nurse. It's done me good, having a bit of a chat. Nobody has time to talk to an old woman nowadays.'

'We must do it again,' Maudie told her.

★ ★ ★

'You must have a cup of tea before you go on your way, Nurse!' Phyllis Green, too, was someone who could benefit from a gossipy chat with another woman.

'Thank you very much. I don't mind if I do!'

'How did you find Her Upstairs today, Nurse?'

'Much brighter, actually. She's been telling me about her family. Speaking of which, she tells me she has a daughter over at Midvale.'

'Yes, that's right. That's our Betty.'

'Well, forgive me for asking, but couldn't she make a home for your mother-in-law to free up a bit of space here, if only temporarily while Brian and Mae are with you?'

'Poor Betty has her own troubles, Nurse. An invalid husband and some grown sons who've never left home. Oh, they're all in work, mind you, so she's not short of a bob or two, but that house of hers is groaning at the seams. No, there's no help there.'

'And what about Fred? I gather he died

a year or two back. Did he leave a widow, or children?'

'Fred? No, not him. A confirmed bachelor all his life, was our Fred.'

★   ★   ★

'If you'll excuse my saying so, Nurse, I think all this business has gone to your head a bit.' Mrs Blunt looked rather put out, and Maudie hastened to soothe her ruffled feathers.

'No, of course I don't believe that Fanny Green buried her baby out in that field!'

'Then what are you saying, exactly?'

'I just want to be able to rule her out, that's all. Dick says that's the essence of good police work. You rule out all the possibilities and then look at what's left.'

'And have you thought what you'll do if the old lady is guilty? Will you turn her over to the law and have her carted off to jail? You might be wise to let well alone.'

'All I want to do is have a look in the church registers, just for my own satisfaction,' Maudie explained.

'And that's another thing. Harold does not permit people to search the registers within the past hundred years, for reasons of privacy. There could be things that people wouldn't want made known — such as births out of wedlock, for instance.'

'And nobody is more likely to keep those secrets than me,' Maudie said. 'I probably know more about the hidden lives of this parish than anyone else, and I'd never blab. Nursing ethics, you see! Well, far be it from me to ask the vicar to go against his principles, but couldn't you have a little peek at the records, just to keep me quiet?' She directed a winning smile at her friend, baring all her teeth.

Despite herself, Mrs Blunt laughed. 'All right, Nurse! No promises, mind, but I'll think about it.'

* * *

Maudie walked home, humming to herself, but her cheerful mood soon evaporated. As she neared the cottage she noticed a man bending over the lavender bushes, bent almost double. Was he in pain? Suffering a heart attack, perhaps, and trying to get help? She quickened her pace, wishing she had been at home when he arrived.

At her approach he straightened up, and she saw to her horror that he had a bright red sign in his hand. 'For Sale', it read. Her heart skipped a beat.

'What do you think you're doing?' she snapped. She had never seen this man before in her life.

'Can't you see? Putting up this sign, that's what I'm doing, missus.'

'But this is my house, and I haven't authorized this!'

'I don't know nothing about that, missus. They told me to come and put up this here sign, and that's what I'm doing. Now, you'd better stand well back while I swing this hammer, or it might catch you a nasty one and then we'd all be in trouble.'

Fuming, she fled into the house, slamming the door behind her. There was no sign of Dick. When she was sure the man had gone, she went outside again;

and, after giving several tugs on the offending sign, managed to pull it out of the ground. 'Take that!' she shouted, throwing it into the shrubbery.

She knew it was only a temporary respite. The parish council owned her beloved cottage. Cruel and unfair though it was, they had the right to dispose of it as they saw fit. She was only making a fool of herself by removing the sign. Swallowing a sob, she retrieved it from among the lilacs and shoved it back into the hole, where it swayed drunkenly.

This was a fine reward for all her years of faithful service to the people of Llandyfan. Someday soon, someone with more money than sense would come along and buy the cottage, and then she and Dick would be out in the cold — homeless.

20

One morning not long afterwards, Maudie was returning home after a long and difficult confinement. For a while she had been tempted to call Dr Dean to come, but then nature and perhaps her guardian angel had decided to cooperate; and, with the assistance of the patient's mother, she had brought a beautiful little baby girl into the world. Pain and fear had been replaced by joy and thanksgiving, and by the time that Maudie saw fit to leave, the morning was half gone.

As she passed the Copper Kettle, the aroma of coffee drew her inside. There was really no reason for her to go home. Dick would have left for work long since, and she was in no mood to cook breakfast for herself. Coffee and a cream doughnut would hit the spot nicely; or a Chelsea bun, sticky with raisins and syrup. Or perhaps a doughnut *and* a Chelsea bun?

The night she'd just had called for some reward.

There were not many people in the little tearoom at that hour of the day. The elderly women who met there on a regular basis were still at home performing various little tasks, and there were no ramblers or tourists passing through on a weekday morning. Maudie recognized Nurse Gregg, seated at a table in the corner, slumped over with her back to the door.

'May I join you, Nurse?'

The girl looked up in surprise.

'Oh, it's you, Nurse. Yes, please do.' Not the most effusive welcome in the world, but it gave Maudie an opening. She squeezed herself between the table and the wall, feeling her way onto the unoccupied chair.

'Is anything wrong? You don't look too cheerful,' Maudie ventured.

'Of course there's nothing wrong!' the girl snapped, but great tears welled up in her eyes and rolled down her cheeks. 'Oh, who am I kidding? I hate nursing, that's all! I absolutely hate nursing!'

At that moment the elderly waitress came up to take Maudie's order. '*Café au lait*, please, Mary, and a jam doughnut; and a repeat order of whatever Nurse Gregg is having.'

'Pot of tea and a custard slice, Nurse.'

'A custard slice sounds lovely. You'd better bring one for me as well.'

'Will that be instead of the doughnut, or as well as?'

Maudie grinned up at the older woman, who seemed to have been working at the Copper Kettle forever. 'You know me better than that, Mary! I've been up all night and I need a little nourishment!'

By the time her order arrived, the other patrons had left, and the two nurses were alone in the tearoom. Maudie looked around her, feeling that time seemed to have stood still here. She had been coming to the Copper Kettle for years, and nothing ever changed: the checked gingham tablecloths, the flower prints on the walls, the scuffed lino on the floor. Only the flowers in the bud vases varied, according to the seasons. Today they held

Michaelmas daisies.

Melanie Gregg poked at her pastry with her fork, not speaking. Her face was stained with the tears she hadn't attempted to wipe away.

'You were saying something about hating nursing,' Maudie prompted. 'Why is that? Has something happened to upset you since you've come to Llandyfan?'

The girl shrugged and did not reply.

'Perhaps district nursing hasn't turned out as well as you hoped? Come on, girl, surely you can tell me? It can't be any big secret! You are still very young; if you don't enjoy nursing, why don't you give it up and go into some other line of work?'

'You don't know my parents!' the girl said sullenly.

'Well, no, I don't, but I'm sure they want you to be happy. Can't you discuss it with them?'

'They wouldn't listen!' the girl pouted; and then it all came pouring out, like a spring that has been dammed up by winter ice and is now free to find its own path again.

'Mum always wanted to be a nurse,

and she actually applied to a hospital for training, but they wouldn't take her. She was told she'd outgrown her strength, whatever that meant. I suppose she was anaemic or something, unless she didn't look hardy enough to cope with the rigours of nursing. So, from the time I was tiny, she brought me up to believe that I was going to be a nurse, too.'

'And what were your thoughts on that? Did you have ambitions to do something else?'

'Well, when I was about six I wanted to be a ballerina, but that was a non-starter. We didn't have the money for lessons.'

'I meant a sensible ambition, when you were older, in high school; when your friends were talking about their future lives.'

'There didn't seem to be much choice. They all wanted to be nurses or teachers or secretaries, just to fill in the time until the right man came along. So when Mum told me it was time to apply to nursing school I did what she said. When I went for my interview with the matron and she asked me why I wanted to be a nurse, I told her I just thought it was a good job to have until I got married. I thought if I didn't go on about wanting to help humanity or something, like Florence Nightingale, she'd turn me down; but she seemed pleased, and said that the nursing profession is no place for girls who don't have their feet on the ground.'

'So, I gather that you took your training, and managed to qualify as a State Registered Nurse. That's worth a great deal.'

'That's right. I knuckled under and did what I was told and I managed to survive the three years. I didn't win any medals, but I squeaked through the exams, and here I am.'

'But if you don't like it here, why do you stay?'

'Because I don't know where else to go. I can't go back to the hospital because there aren't any vacancies.'

This made sense to Maudie, who assumed that conditions in most big hospitals were much the same as in the one where she herself had trained, They probably took in six dozen trainees each year, and those girls performed much of the work, under the leadership of a couple of staff nurses in each ward, presided over by ward sisters. Only a few members of each graduating set were offered permanent positions there, while the rest had to go on to other things.

Some girls got married; some went on to further training in midwifery; some found posts in nursing homes or private hospitals; others joined Queen Alexandra's Royal Army Nursing Corps, or sought jobs abroad. For the qualified nurse, the world was her oyster.

'I understand that you've had a bit of difficulty keeping up with your appointments,' she said, choosing her words with care. 'Would you like to tell me about that?'

Nurse Gregg blushed. 'Oh, there were a couple of misunderstandings, that's all they were. I was supposed to show a woman how to make a poultice, but I meant I would do it at the surgery, and she thought I was going to her home instead.'

'And Mr Dobb, the man with the stroke?'

'His wife said her neighbour would come in to help her, and they could manage perfectly well without me. The trouble was, the neighbour got called away, and the daughter phoned through to the newsagent's up the end of our street and left a message for me to come. He sent a boy to let me know, but unfortunately he didn't write it down, so by the time Auntie tried to pass on the message to me, it was hopelessly garbled. Something about a man who couldn't find his clogs, if you please!'

'Something will have to be done about this,' Maudie said severely. 'I'm not blaming you, Nurse, but this slipshod manner of communication is not good enough. I advise you to speak to Dr Dean at once, and get him to put pressure on the GPO to have a telephone installed at your aunt's house immediately.'

Melanie Gregg turned as red as the beetroot Maudie detested so much. 'I don't want to speak to that man again!'

'I'm afraid you'll have to, my dear. He

happens to be our superior.'

'Then you tell him. Won't you, please?'

'Has Dr Dean done something to upset you, Nurse?' Maudie recalled what June Faber had said to Mrs Blunt about seeing the pair together.

'Not exactly. Oh, I feel such a fool!'

21

'So that's it, really,' Maudie told Mrs Blunt. 'More or less a chapter of accidents. Where Nurse Gregg made her mistake was in not apologizing to the patients she inadvertently missed, whether or not she was actually at fault. One way or another, the system let them down. The best we can do is insist that Mrs Faber's house be put on the phone, and after that it's up to Nurse Gregg to pull her weight.'

'What did you advise her to do in the end?'

'I pointed out that she is under contract, and if I were her I'd give it my very best effort until the term expires. After that, she should decide what to do with her life and somehow find the courage to face her parents with it. She is over twenty-one, after all. They no longer have any say in the matter.'

'I always feel it's a great mistake when

parents try to live vicariously through their children, or try to force them into a career they are not fitted for.'

'Oh, well, I've had my say. Let's hope she pays attention. Speaking of which, my words of wisdom regarding Dr Dean were less well-received!'

'Just what is the story there?'

Maudie sighed. 'Reading between the lines, I think that her plan B, if I can put it that way, is to get married and forget about nursing. And who better to choose for a husband than a doctor? As a former nurse she will understand him, and possibly be a help to him in his work.

'Well, Nurse Gregg came to Llandyfan and found herself answerable to our Dr Dean. Personable, well-established in his profession — and, above all, single! Who can blame her if she felt attracted to him? And I gather that he made himself quite pleasant to her — which isn't always the case in his attitude to nurses, as I know to my cost! On one occasion he even ran her home in his car after she'd missed her bus, when she'd been in Midvale going over her case notes with him.'

'Very convenient!'

'In return, she invited him out on a picnic — that was probably the occasion Mrs Faber mentioned to you, when he picked her up at the house — but unfortunately it all went wrong. Our Dr Dean spent the whole afternoon talking about Valerie, trying to pick Nurse Gregg's brains as to how he should handle a certain situation.'

'Who is Valerie? Do we know her?'

'Apparently not. She is another doctor, and the love of Donald Dean's life. He has proposed marriage to her, and she's prepared to consider it, but only if he goes with her to Toronto, where she has accepted a post at a big hospital.'

'Poor Nurse Gregg. I hope she'll recover.'

'I think her hope is that if he gives Valerie the push, he'll fall for Melanie on the rebound, and they will live happily ever after. I suppose it could happen.'

'What it is to be young and in love,' Mrs Blunt murmured. 'Never mind, she has plenty of time to find the right man. Look at you, Nurse. I don't mean to imply that you are — er — middle-aged; but here you are, not in the first flush of youth, recently happily married for the first time. You are an example to us all.'

'Yes,' Maudie said, 'I am well aware of how lucky I am. However, this happy marriage may not last for much longer unless I go home immediately and put the potatoes on. Just look at the time! If my marriage collapses I shall have you to blame, keeping me here gossiping when I should be about my wifely chores.'

'Get along with you!' Mrs Blunt said, laughing. 'You know you just couldn't wait to spill the beans.'

* * *

'I've had a word with Sam Barrow,' Dick announced, when he had scraped the last smear of custard from his bowl.

'Oh, yes? Who might he be?'

'An old mate from when I was on the darts team at the Spread Eagle in Midvale. He works for an estate agent now. I asked him what he thinks this cottage is worth on the open market, and he says that without actually coming and measuring up, his guess would be somewhere in the region of twelve hundred pounds.'

'Twelve hundred! But that's a far cry from the three thousand quid the council are asking.'

'Not only that, but at that rate, you and I have a much better chance of raising the dosh!'

Hope flared up in Maudie for a moment, only to fade again like a spent Roman candle falling to earth. 'I'm sure that won't impress the council when somebody else comes along with two thousand more in their hot little hands.'

'But don't you see, Maudie, if we can present them with a *fait accompli* they may just jump at it? Surely it's worth a try. If we don't act soon, people will start coming to view the place, and when they see how snug you've made it they won't be able to resist.'

'I shall borrow Perkin from the vicarage and tell people we need a good mouser because the place is simply overrun with vermin. That should put a few of them off. And if that doesn't work, we can say the place is haunted.'

'It's all very well to joke about it, my love,' Dick said, 'but that won't help us in the end. We have to come up with a strategic plan.'

'I suppose we could always have a word with the editor of The Midvale Chronicle. He's had plenty of mileage out of me in the past, with the murders and whatnot. He could run a photo of me, bleating about being turned out of my home after all these years of faithful service,' Maudie said. 'Perhaps it would shame the parish council into rethinking the situation.'

'And how do you think that would make me look?' Dick asked, not altogether sure if his wife meant what she said, or if it was only one of her humorous asides. 'A man with a good job who can't even put a roof over his wife's head? No, old girl; if we have to leave here we'll go with heads held high and a stiff upper lip. Have you forgotten the spirit that turned the tide at Dunkirk?'

So that evening the Bryants got out

their post office savings books and did their sums once again. Dick felt that with a lot of scrimping and saving they might be able to obtain a mortgage based on a final price of twelve hundred pounds, and Maudie went along with that because she didn't want to discourage him. Privately, she felt that he was being overly optimistic, and it might be better if they faced facts now and started to let go of their dream.

She would have a word with Dora Frost at the Royal Oak. The pub was actually an old coaching inn, and the landlord occasionally let rooms to visitors. Could one of the larger ones be made available to the Bryants? There was, of course, the problem of what to do with their furniture and their growing number of joint possessions: all that would have to go into storage somewhere which would cost money — money that could be put to better use in buying a home of their own. Still, there was no use in moaning. As long as they were together, that was all that really mattered, wasn't it?

22

Maudie opened the door to find Mrs Blunt on the doorstep, looking anxiously over her shoulder.

'Can I come in? I don't want Harold to know where I am. As it is, I've had a most difficult time going through the parish registers without him knowing what I'm up to.'

'And have you uncovered anything exciting?' Maudie asked, leading the way to the kitchen. 'Tea? Bovril?'

'No, thanks. I can't stop long. He thinks I've just slipped out to post a letter.'

'Don't keep me in suspense, then! What have you found?'

'Nothing, really. What I mean is, when it comes to Mrs Green's family, everything is as it should be. I found the baptisms of all her babies, as well as a note in the margin recording that Martin was killed in action at Ypres and buried out there. And there is a record of baby

Alice's death and burial, so she is definitely not the mystery baby.'

'Drat!'

'What took me so long is that I went through every entry throughout the 1880s and 1890s, just in case there was an extra birth recorded that would fit your theory, but there isn't anything. So that's it, I'm afraid.'

'Yes, back to square one.'

'Now, I must dash. I've left a stew cooking on the stove and I can't trust Harold to keep an eye on it. As usual, he's struggling with a sermon, and his head is in the clouds.'

'Hang on a minute,' Maudie said. 'I think I'd better find out more about the manor estate — who lived there when Fanny Green was a young bride, and so on. Do you think the Midvale library would have anything on file?'

'Why don't you start with Cora Beasley? She may have documents dealing with the place. Now really, Nurse, I must go!' The vicar's wife left by the back door, leaving Maudie to mull over what she had been told.

Cora Beasley was the nearest thing to the lady of the manor that Llandyfan was likely to get. Her huge house and the surrounding acreage had been purchased years ago by her late father-in-law, a wealthy Victorian industrialist. Mrs Beasley had come there as a young bride, and now, years later, she was an equally wealthy widow who was looked up to by the socially conscious residents of the parish.

There was rarely a committee on which she did not serve, and she was generous in handing out largesse to worthy causes. When it came to finding someone to open the church fete, or to announce the start of Boy Scout Bob-a-Job week, it was always Mrs Beasley's name that came to mind first.

It was Cora Beasley who had provided both the location and the funding for the doctor's surgery in the former gatehouse on the estate. Admittedly, she had done this with her nephew in mind, but that was beside the point. It benefited all the local patients, who would otherwise have had to travel the twelve miles to Midvale by bus to consult the doctor.

It was not her fault that Dr Lennox, who was in partnership with Dr Dean at Midvale, should have been wrongfully accused of murder and temporarily kept in prison. Thanks to Maudie he had been proved innocent, but his aunt had seen that it would not do for him to return to work in Llandyfan. Country people tended to be suspicious by nature when it came to incomers, and more than one person had been heard to mutter 'No smoke without fire'. So the surgery stood idle for much of the time, except when Nurse Gregg held clinic days there.

★ ★ ★

Mrs Beasley was only too happy to talk to Maudie about her beloved home. 'Anything that's written down is in my safety deposit box at the bank,' she said. 'I can arrange to get the documents out for you if you are interested in that sort of thing, but I can probably answer most of your questions myself. What is it you'd like to know, Nurse?'

'I've been wondering about the family who owned the place before you,' Maudie said. 'When did they come here? When was the house built? That sort of thing.'

'Ah, yes. Well, my father-in-law bought it from a titled family called Helmes. That would be back in 1862 when old Lord Roderick died.'

'I wonder why they had to sell?' Maudie asked, her imagination running riot. 'Did Lord Roderick gamble away all his money, or something?'

Mrs Beasley laughed. 'Really, Nurse, you ought to be writing books! No, it was something quite ordinary. There was only one son, among several daughters, and the title died out when the boy was killed at the Crimea. I think that Lady Victoria — she was his mother — must have been quite elderly by the time she was widowed, and she probably didn't have the heart to carry on alone with her son gone. So she sold the place to Mr Beasley.'

'I see.' Maudie wanted to ask if the

documents might shed any light on the mystery baby, but she couldn't think how to bring the subject up without somehow casting suspicion on Mr Beasley senior. However, Mrs Beasley was too clever for her.

'You want to find out if that baby has any connection to the Helmes family, don't you, Nurse,' she said, with a slight smile on her lips. 'Don't bother to deny it! I'd very much like to know the answer to that myself. In fact, I've lain awake these past few nights trying to puzzle it out!'

It took Maudie a few moments to recover from the surprise, but then she realized she'd been given an opportunity that might not come again. Mrs Beasley had been so distressed by the events that had taken place at her home a year earlier — one nephew falsely accused and another actually proved to be a murderer — that she'd declared her intention to sell up and moved away. Then she had decided to stay and face the community; and, in the main, mindful of her past good works, people had been supportive of her and her distress had begun to fade.

However, she was getting on a bit, and who knew when she might change her mind and take herself off to a private nursing home?

'You mentioned daughters,' Maudie said. 'What became of them all?'

'Let me see, now. I believe they were Miss Amelia, Miss Vicky, Miss Beatrice and Miss Sophie. Or were they Honourables? I'm never too sure about what you're supposed to call a lord's daughters. It depends on what sort of lord, I suppose. As far as I know, they all married and went elsewhere to live. The parish registers would show that, if Mr Blunt would give you permission to leaf through them.'

Maudie blushed. 'Is it possible that one of them had a baby she couldn't acknowledge?'

'If she got involved with a groom or something, you mean? I'm unable to answer that, but if that happened I'd imagine the wanton girl would be sent away from home to have the child in seclusion. If it died it would hardly be sent home for burial in the family plot, and it certainly wouldn't have been put in a corner of George Bull's field! Not that George Bull had it then, but you know what I mean.'

There was no more to be said for the moment, so when Mrs Beasley had agreed to retrieve the estate documents from the bank, Maudie set out to cycle the mile back to the village. While their conversation was fresh in her mind, she thought she might as well go into the churchyard and have a look at the Helmes family graves.

Their plot lay in the older section at the back of the cemetery, shaded by some ancient yews. The graves were surrounded by a sturdy wrought-iron fence — almost as if in death, as in life, the ordinary folk of the village were meant to keep their distance from their betters. The gate creaked when Maudie let herself into the enclosure, almost as if it was warning those who lay there of her approach.

She soon found the headstone of Lord Roderick Helmes, 1785 to 1862, and his beloved wife, Lady Victoria Gray, 1792 to 1865. Of their four daughters there was no sign; probably, as Mrs Beasley had suggested, they had gone away when they married and now lay beside their husbands in some other place. She glanced at a number of ancient stones that probably marked the last resting place of other Helmes ancestors, but they were covered in lichen and the inscriptions were too hard to read.

Maudie then went into the church, where she knew that there were some memorial tablets on the walls. For years she had let her glance rest idly on them while she was sitting quietly in her pew, but had never been interested enough to look at them more closely. Although St. John's was very old, it wasn't the sort of church where you found the tombs with effigies of men in amour, with their legs crossed to show they had been on crusade. Now it was time to pay closer attention.

23

Old Mrs Green never did see her ninetieth birthday, as she had expected to do. She passed away quietly in her sleep, at home, in her own bed, as she would have wished.

'I went up to her with a cup of tea and I found her lying there, quite peacefully, gone from this world,' Phyllis told Maudie. 'I wondered why she hadn't been calling down and rapping on the floor with her stick; but the baby had us up half the night, and I was just grateful for the bit of a break so I didn't go up as early as usual. Poor old soul! I feel guilty now for thinking her a nuisance.'

'You did your best,' Maudie told her. 'That's all any of us can do in the end. I suppose she'll be buried at St. John's?'

'That's right. She wanted to be laid to rest beside her husband. Josh and I will be there too, when our time comes.'

'Well, if there's anything I can do to help . . . '

'You've helped me to lay her out, and the doctor and the undertaker have already been notified, so I can't think of anything else you could do at the moment. I've sent one of the boys to find Josh and bring him home from work; his rheumatics were playing him up this morning so he'll be glad of a day off, even if it is on account of bad news. Someone will have to get a message to Betty at Midvale, though, and she's not on the phone. I suppose I could send the boy over there on the bus. I don't like to ask Dr Dean to go and break the news to her.'

'I could probably get in touch with Dick,' Maudie told her. 'He's supposed to be at the police station there today. I'm sure he could go in search of her. The police are used to breaking bad news to people, unfortunately.'

'Well, if you think your hubby wouldn't mind . . . '

'I'm sure he'd be glad to help, Mrs Green.'

'That's one less thing to worry about, then. Thanks, Nurse! All I have left to do now then is write to Josh's brothers in Australia, if I can lay my hands on an address for them. They won't be coming to the funeral, of course; it's too far to travel, never mind that they couldn't get here in time, sailing all that way on a ship.'

Nodding in agreement, Maudie reflected how odd it was that they still talked about 'sailing' on a ship when the days of sail were long past, unless it had to do with small pleasure craft. Apparently, that was not the only thing that was passing from the world as they knew it, for Phyllis went on to point out that her mother-in-law had been one of the last of her generation in the district. All her old cronies had gone before her, and hardly any of her contemporaries were left to attend her funeral.

★ ★ ★

So the elderly grandmother was gone. Well, she had had a good innings, and

Maudie suspected that she hadn't been all that sorry to go. Spending your days alone in a room under the eaves, with nothing to do and no strength to speak of, was not much of a life; and knowing you were a burden to others did not make your lot any easier to bear. And had Fanny realized that she was becoming senile, with the loss of dignity that might involve?

Dick, when he came home that evening, confirmed that he had been able to find Betty Green — Mrs Lewis as she was now — and had informed her of her mother's death.

'Was she very upset?' Maudie wondered.

'She shed a few tears, but I made her a brew and she cheered up a bit in the end. There's another one with a long row to hoe, Maudie. She's got a husband sitting there in a wheelchair, and a house full of grown children who've had to move back home because they've nowhere else to go. One son hasn't been able to find a job since he was demobbed from the army five years ago, and a daughter who used to work in munitions was laid off when the war ended and told to go back to the kitchen. I came away thinking how lucky we are.'

★ ★ ★

On the day of Mrs Green's funeral, Maudie was seated in the church in plenty of time. She always made a point of attending any local funeral having to do with the families of her patients, which all boiled down to the fact that she hardly ever missed one.

The coffin was carried in by the required six pallbearers, all dressed in sober black. Maudie recognized Brian Green and three shorter and thinner versions of himself, probably his younger brothers. The tallest one was wearing trousers that were much too short for him, so his ankles were clearly visible, covered in fluorescent green socks. Maudie surmised that the trousers were borrowed for the occasion.

The other pallbearers were also fairly youthful-looking men who bore a vague resemblance to the Green boys. The sons of their Aunt Betty, perhaps? The chief mourners included Josh and Phyllis, the former appearing slightly lame, and a gaunt woman pushing a man in a wheelchair down the aisle. These were the Lewises, perhaps. How on earth had they managed to get the poor man the twelve miles from Midvale if he couldn't walk? The wheelchair was a sturdy old-fashioned apparatus, the type that didn't fold for easy transportation. All this pleasant conjecture kept Maudie happy until the vicar arrived and the service began.

When the small congregation gathered at the graveside, Maudie stood well back, not wishing to intrude on the family's grief. They knew who she was; if they wished to speak to her afterwards, that was up to them. But when the woman she believed to be Betty Lewis suddenly uttered a strangled cry and doubled over, she hurried forward to give assistance.

'Stand back, everyone, please! Give her room to breathe.' She helped the woman to sit down on a nearby bench while the other mourners looked on in consternation. The vicar hesitated for a moment and then carried on.

'I'll be all right,' the woman whispered, but to Maudie's trained eye she certainly appeared far from well. Phyllis Green came to them when the service was over, looking worried.

'We're going to the parish hall now, Betty. There will be tea and a sandwich waiting for us. Can you make it that far? A cup of tea may be just what you need.'

'I don't think so,' her sister-in-law replied in a weak little voice.

'I don't know how we can manage,' Phyllis said, turning to Maudie. 'We have to go and chat with people; thank them for coming and that. I suppose Betty really needs to go home and lie down, but transportation is the problem. Her neighbour brought them from Midvale in his grocer's van; because of her man's wheelchair, you see. He had to get back to see to his business and he won't be returning to pick them up until later in the day. I suppose we could send her back in a taxi, but that will cost the earth, and there's nobody back at the house to see to her if she comes over queer.'

'I've said I'm all right, haven't I? I just don't think I could face that lot, that's all.'

Maudie, noticing that the colour was coming back into the woman's face, made a decision. 'My home is just over the way, there, Mrs Lewis. Do you think you could manage to walk that far? You could sit quietly there until your friend comes to take you home, or you could have a nice lie-down if you prefer.'

'That's right,' Phyllis said, beaming with relief, 'you go with Nurse. We'll make sure your hubby is all right.'

So Maudie and her patient slowly made their way to the cottage, where bed rest was offered and refused, and a strong brew of tea was made and accepted. Betty Lewis was silent at first, but under Maudie's gentle questioning she seemed to relax, chattering away about her husband and children and the life they led in Midvale. Then it hit home once again that her mother had just been laid to rest, and she seemed to be overcome with guilt and remorse.

'Poor Mother! I should have done more for her, but I left it all to Phyllis!'

'I'm sure you have nothing to reproach yourself with,' Maudie soothed. 'You have an invalid husband to care for — and a houseful of people to cook and clean for, too. One woman can only do so much. And it isn't as if Mrs Green was left alone somewhere, unable to fend for herself. She had Phyllis and her family to look after her, didn't she?'

'But I should have made the time to go and see her. I can't remember the last time I came over to Llandyfan. She loved to talk about the old days, you know. All I had to do was listen, but I couldn't even be bothered to do that.'

Maudie patted the grieving woman on the shoulder. 'I'm sure she had plenty of stories to tell when you were young. She was born into a different world, in the middle of the old Queen's reign.'

Betty's expression softened. 'She did tell me a lot of strange things when I was quite small. I'm the only girl in the family, you see, apart from a baby sister who died, and I suppose she felt closer to me in some ways than the boys. I wish now I'd paid more attention, but you know what it's like when you're young — it all goes in one ear and out the other!'

Maudie pricked up her own ears on hearing that! 'What sort of things, Mrs Lewis? Fairy tales, perhaps, or reminisces of Llandyfan in the old days? I'm quite interested in local history myself, not having been born and bred in these parts.'

Betty Lewis absent-mindedly reached out for another custard cream. 'Oh, the usual things, I suppose; like Cinderella, Goldilocks and the Three Bears . . . And then there were some tales I can vaguely remember about the family up at the manor. Looking back, I don't know if they were true stories or maybe things she made up as she went along, to entertain me, like.

'There was one yarn in particular she used to tell, about the son of the house and a maid they had up there. Something about them falling in love, only they couldn't be wed because he was going to inherit the estate and a title, and she was just a simple village girl. Perhaps it really happened, or maybe there was nothing to it, and poor old Mum was thinking of something she'd read in a penny novelette. She could read and write, you know, Mum could. She was really proud of that. Not too many girls had much schooling in her day, but somehow her parents managed to find the penny a week it cost to send her to school.'

Maudie was about to probe into this story when there was a rap on the back door and she opened it to find one of the Green boys squinting down at her. 'Mum says the van is here to take you back, Auntie Bet, and if you don't want to be left behind you'd better come now.'

'You just run back and tell the driver to come here,' Maudie told him. 'Mrs Lewis will meet him at the front door. It doesn't make sense for her to trek all across the graveyard when they'll be going right past here on their way home.'

'Okey-dokey, Missus!' The gangly teen-ager sped off, obviously happy to be freed from the unwelcome constraints of the day.

24

'I think I may have got to the bottom of our mystery,' Maudie told Dick. They were busily scrubbing down bathroom walls in an effort to make the place presentable when prospective buyers called to see the cottage. The tile had become dingy-looking from years of steam and everyday wear, and some of the grouting needed to be replaced. It wasn't that Maudie wanted to make it more attractive for the benefit of the parish council, but she couldn't have strangers thinking she was a poor housewife. As a nurse, she would be expected to have a home that was particularly hygienic.

The front door needed painting and there was a crack in the scullery window; but, as Dick said, there was no point in going overboard. If the council wanted those things upgrading, let them pay a workman to do it.

'The baby, you mean?' Dick murmured now, standing back to admire his handiwork.

'Of course the baby! Well, from what I gathered from Mrs Lewis, it was just the old, old story. Lord of the manor takes advantage of a poor servant girl and gets her with child.'

'And?'

'That's it, I suppose. Of course, old Mrs Green had to put a more romantic spin on it. The couple were in love, but they couldn't marry because of class distinction.'

'Hmm. Do you think we ought to do something about that damp stain on the ceiling?'

'No. What do you think about what I've just said?'

Dick shrugged. 'It could be true, I suppose. Who's to tell after all this time? That still doesn't explain what happened to the baby, or why it was buried in the field. Did the girl do away with the baby to hide her shame?'

'If she was still in Llandyfan when the baby came to term, she could hardly have kept her condition hidden! And if it was several months old when it died, as your police surgeon says, why weren't there questions asked about what had become of it?'

'Perhaps there were,' Dick said.

'And perhaps there weren't. People in country places have long memories.'

'So what? The girl may well have gone somewhere else, Maudie. Didn't girls in trouble always get sent away to help an auntie or a grandmother?'

'Then how did the baby end up being buried here?'

'We may never find the answer to that question. What I do know is, I have a raging thirst. Will you put the kettle on, or shall I?'

★ ★ ★

The first people who came to inspect the house were a middle-aged couple who arrived in an imposing Lanchester car. The wife, wearing a smart tweed costume and pearls, looked Maudie up and down for a long moment before speaking.

'Yes, can I help you?'

'Possibly. Is your mistress at home?'

It took Maudie a few seconds to grasp what was being implied. She had her head tied up in a turban, and she was wearing a frayed pinny and holding a mop; but this was a country cottage, not a stately home, and not the sort of place that employed resident servants. Well, two could play at that game!

'I'm sorry, Madam, the mistress has gone out and she didn't say when she might be back,' she murmured, trying to look like a version of Worzel Gummidge, the talking scarecrow of the popular children's books.

'Then perhaps you'll be so good as to show us round,' the awful woman said.

'Round, Madam?' Maudie let her mouth drop open.

'We wish to inspect the premises. This cottage is for sale, isn't it? At least, that is what the sign on the lawn seems to indicate.'

'I don't know, Madam, I'm sure.'

'My husband is in the car. I'll just call him over, shall I, and we'll have a quick pop around. There is no need to keep you from your work. If we have any questions we'll drop in at the house agent's office afterwards.' She turned to signal to the man who was waiting in the car.

Maudie had had enough of this. 'I'm sorry, Madam, but the mistress has given me strict orders not to let anyone in while she is away. For all I know you could be con artists, working in pairs. I've heard about people like you. You'll keep me talking while your partner nips upstairs looking for valuables to steal. Perhaps you should make an appointment to view, as it suggests on the board outside.'

'Well, really!' The woman's face was purple with rage now, and Maudie hoped she wasn't about to have a stroke on the spot. 'This is an outrage! I shall report this, you see if I don't.'

'Yes, Madam. Good morning!' Maudie closed the door firmly. Moments later, she heard the car drive away.

★　★　★

'So that's what I said,' Maudie told Mrs Blunt, who had called round with a copy of the parish magazine.

'Oh, Nurse! Do you think you should have done that? What if she *does* complain? It certainly won't endear you to Councillor Reeves and company.'

'Perhaps not,' said Maudie, who by now was feeling slightly guilty. 'People like her get my back up, that's all. Why should she speak to me as if I don't matter, just because she thought I was the charwoman? And I know I was playing the fool, but it pays to be careful. You do hear of people going around robbing houses like that.'

'But possibly not people driving Lanchesters,' Mrs Blunt said mildly.

'Ah, now that's where you're wrong. First they go to a local car salesroom, pretending to buy an expensive car. They take it for a test drive. They go straight to the house they've already earmarked and they insist on viewing it. The householder sees the car, thinks they must be people of means, and lets them inside. One of the pair then keeps her talking while the other roams around pocketing anything that isn't nailed down.'

'You've been reading too many who-dunnits, Nurse.'

'Yes, I probably have, but they're a good education when it comes to seeing through my fellow man — or woman, as the case may be. Miss Marple solves her crimes by understanding human nature, doesn't she!'

'Very well, Nurse, you win! But you can't go on like this you know.'

'I realize that, but I shall visit the house agent and insist that people come to view the house by appointment only. It's for their own benefit, you know. It would save people a wasted trip, calling when there is nobody home. We do go out to work, you know!'

★ ★ ★

Maudie received a phone call from Cora Beasley, inviting her to come for tea. 'I've been to the bank and I want to let you see those estate papers I told you about. Would you like to come at about three or half-past?'

'Yes, I would, please, if I don't get any more interruptions. People are wanting to view the house, and I can't seem to get on at all.'

Despite everything, Maudie managed to arrive at the manor house by three-fifteen, when Mrs Beasley greeted her with some surprise.

'Here you are after all, Nurse! You had me a bit muddled when we spoke earlier. Why would people want to view the house, as you put it? Perhaps some artist wishes to paint the exterior to put on the lid of a chocolate box or something? I can't imagine why. It's a good little cottage but less than outstanding to look at.'

Maudie grimaced. 'Oh, haven't you heard? The parish council has plans to sell it, and whenever a suitable buyer comes along we'll have to move out.'

'But it's your home!'

'Yes, but of course we don't own it. We'd love to buy it ourselves, but I'm afraid we'll be outbid by someone with more money than we can raise. Dick feels we can get a mortgage, but of course my income won't count, so that limits our chances considerably.'

'And where will you go, Nurse?'

'Ah, now, that's the problem. There isn't anywhere we can rent, and I just don't feel like moving into one room at the Royal Oak! Dick isn't all that worried, because his work takes in a wide area, and he does have a car now. He says we can probably find somewhere away from Llandyfan. Of course, it means that I'll have to give up the job here, which will be a wrench after all this time, but I am married now and my place is with my husband.'

'Of course; but, oh dear! What will our mothers and babies do without you?' Mrs Beasley hesitated. 'I could always put the pair of you up here, Nurse. Heaven knows this house is big enough, and since my nephew left there's nobody here but my maid and myself. We must give it some thought.'

'That is very generous of you,' Maudie murmured.

25

Sitting at the enormous walnut dining table with the extra leaf inserted in the middle, Maudie tried to conceal her impatience as Mrs Beasley slowly skimmed each document before passing it over to her. She longed to plunge her arms into the heavy cardboard file boxes, hunting for clues to aid in her quest, but had no wish to appear rude.

A lot of the papers were useless for her purposes, all couched in legal jargon. Leases and tenancies and lands bought and sold. Fields and woodlands described in terms of roods and acreages, chains and furlongs. A social historian might have found it interesting, and Mrs Beasley could be forgiven for taking an interest in the estate which had come to her through marriage. To Maudie, it was of no interest whatsoever. She shuffled on her hard chair, longing to get up and walk about, but afraid of breaking the spell.

Mrs Beasley might well dust off her hands, saying 'Nothing interesting here,' and prepare to return the boxes to the bank.

'You might like to look at this,' she said instead. Without much hope, Maudie accepted the thin notebook offered to her. It was a child's school exercise book with ruled lines, the sort that had tables and other mathematical information on the back. It turned out to contain someone's attempt at recording a family tree of the Helmes family, the people who had owned the estate before it was sold to Mrs Beasley's father-in-law.

There were a lot of names and dates, although unfortunately very little about the lives and times of the actual people. With a bit of mental arithmetic, Maudie deduced that Victoria Helmes, nee Lady Victoria Gray, had been thirty-eight years old when her only son, Quentin, was born in 1830. As Maudie already knew, there had been four daughters before him. Had Lady Victoria been overtaken by the menopause after that? Or, having done her duty by producing the heir to the title at last, had she taken to her couch to live out her life as a genteel invalid, as so many Victorian ladies did in order to avoid more pregnancies?

'I'm afraid I have to be going,' Maudie said at last, standing up. 'My husband will be home soon, and I've no idea what to make for his tea. Thank you so much for going to all this trouble for me, letting me see your papers.'

'I'm only sorry you didn't find anything helpful, Nurse, but I do find all this quite fascinating. If I come across anything of interest to you, I'll let you know.'

'Thank you very much, Mrs Beasley. I'd appreciate that.'

*   *   *

All the way home, Maudie's mind was working furiously. For want of any better clues, she decided to follow up Mrs Lewis's theory about the son of the house and the servant girl. Quentin Helmes had been born in 1830. If he was a precocious young man, he could have had an affair with a girl at the age of sixteen or seventeen, say, in 1846. According to the memorial tablet in the church he had died in 1854, so that left a span of perhaps eight years during which he could have fathered a child.

What if Quentin had decided to flout convention by marrying the girl he loved? That hardly mattered now. He had gone off to war and been killed, possibly unaware that the girl was expecting his baby. She, poor girl, had died of grief — no, that was too fanciful, even for a Victorian novelette! The baby had been stillborn, and . . .

Maudie Bryant, you're an idiot! she scolded herself. Nobody would think you're a sensible nurse and midwife! It's more likely that the poor girl was taken advantage of by that Quentin Helmes! How often do titled gentleman fall in love with scullery maids, or whatever she was? And we don't even know that the chap had anything at all to do with the mother of the mystery baby whose bones were accidentally dug up by George Bull! Get back into the real world and decide what you're going to give your husband for his tea!

'As far as I know at the moment, I'm going to be working in the Midvale station all day tomorrow,' Dick told Maudie when he was happily digging into sausage and mash and mushy peas. 'What do you have on? If you wanted to go shopping or anything, I'll give you a lift in. If something comes up and I have to leave, you could always catch a bus home, I suppose.'

Maudie was about to say that she was planning to spend the day washing curtains, and then had second thoughts.

'I think I would like a day out; and while I'm there, I can look in on Mrs Lewis and make sure she's all right.'

'Won't the district nurse at Midvale do that?'

'Very possibly, but I think she'd appreciate it if I enquired too. After all, I was able to give assistance when she collapsed at the funeral, and I did know her mother.'

'You do as you like, love. Just be ready to leave home in plenty of time in the morning, all right?'

Maudie was genuinely concerned about Mrs Lewis and eager to offer support. The woman had lost her mother, and the realization would have sunk in by now. She could use a bit of sympathy. At the same time, Maudie wanted to question her further about the story told to her by old Mrs Green. Now she'd had time to think about it, she might have recalled some small detail that would fit into the overall story.

Betty Lewis was surprised and pleased to see Maudie, and the first few minutes were spent in reviewing details of the funeral and introducing her husband, Stan.

'You'll take a cup of coffee, I hope, Nurse. I always make one for myself in time to sit down with *Mrs Dale's Diary*.'

Maudie always listened to the popular drama on the wireless whenever she managed to be at home in the mornings, and it seemed that Stan Lewis enjoyed it too. The three of them were soon sitting enthralled by the latest doings of the Dale family, while enjoying milky coffee and a

Bourbon biscuit.

'I do worry about Jim,' the leading character said when the day's short episode came to an end. Jim was Mrs Dale's husband.

'I wouldn't be without my programme,' Mrs Lewis said. 'You need something to take you out of yourself, if you know what I mean.' This gave Maudie the chance she needed.

'About that story you told me, that came from your mother. Have you by chance remembered any more details? I didn't have time to ask questions because your nephew turned up then.'

Mrs Lewis shook her head. 'As I told you, I was very young at the time — and not noted for paying close attention to what people said to me, or I might have done better at school! And anyway, I don't expect there was any truth to it. Not that Mum would have told a lie, mind you, but it was probably just a fairy story, like Cinderella or some such.'

'Never mind, it was worth a try. I don't suppose you could direct me to any local pensioner who might know more? A woman, preferably. Women always seem to take more of an interest in love stories than men do.'

'I expect you're asking questions a few years too late, Nurse. Anyone who might have known the rights of it would most likely be dead by now.'

'You could try the Midvale Museum,' Stan Lewis said suddenly.

'Do you think they could help?'

'My Stan has been a member of the historical society for years,' his wife said proudly. 'He goes to their meetings whenever he can get someone to push him there in his chair. That curator at the museum is an old miseryguts, but just you mention Stan's name and I'm sure he'll try to help you.'

Stan nodded in agreement. 'I seem to recall they have a box of writings dating from the time of the old queen's Diamond Jubilee. Back in 1897, that was,' he went on, in case Maudie didn't know.

'People made a record of things that happened locally during her reign. You might find something there.'

Thanking them profusely, Maudie went

off in search of the museum, which was located in a former factory on River Street. The curator, who was indeed a crusty old buffer, informed Maudie that they were open on Tuesdays and Thursdays — which was good news, as this was a Thursday! On the other hand, they closed at two o'clock, which meant that she wouldn't have much time to do whatever it was that she wanted to do. They had a fine exhibition of old medical instruments; perhaps she would care to see that?

Maudie explained that she was a nurse, and thus well acquainted with the tools of her profession; what she really wanted to see was the collection of Victorian reminiscences.

'Are you interested in something in particular, Madam? It would take weeks for you to read through the whole collection, and we close in two hours.'

Luckily for Maudie, the curator knew exactly what she was talking about, and where to lay his hands on the artefact in question. Soon she was seated at a large old-fashioned desk with a pile of papers in front of her. The ink was faded and the words hard to decipher, but before she had gone very far she knew she had her hands on a gem.

The writer described herself as a local schoolmistress, Miss Eleanor Sanders, whose family had lived 'in the Llandyfan area since the year dot. This story was told to me by my paternal grandmother, Polly Sanders, who swore me to secrecy during her lifetime because of the trouble her words would have brought on the heads of those involved. All have since passed to their reward, so it can do no harm to record these happenings now.'

In her haste Maudie turned over two pages at once, her gaze falling on the words 'and it was my grandmother who helped to bury little Quentin'. She almost jumped out of her skin when she felt the curator's bony hand on her shoulder, for she had been so engrossed that she hadn't heard him coming.

'I'm sorry, Madam, I must ask you to leave. I'm about to lock up now. You can return on Tuesday if you wish.'

Maudie yelped out a word she would

normally never *dream* of saying aloud. She couldn't possibly let herself be turned away now!

'I beg your pardon, Madam!' The poor man's outraged expression would have caused her to laugh in any other context, but she couldn't back down. This was the Maudie Bryant who had encountered several murderers — and faced up to two of them. She could give no quarter now! If she was forced to retreat, she was determined to go down fighting.

26

'You were lucky the chap didn't show you the door,' Dick said, laughing.

'I really thought he was going to, until I forced him to listen to my story,' Maudie replied. 'I had to stretch the truth a bit and say I was trying to help the police; but he already knew about the discovery of the baby's bones from the story in *The Midvale Chronicle*, so in the end he got quite excited when he heard that his dusty old papers might have actually helped to solve a crime. And I suppose it was a crime, Dick, wasn't it?'

'I don't know enough about the law to say whether it was a criminal offence to bury someone in unhallowed ground in those days; perhaps Mr Blunt is up on that sort of thing. I know that one can't just decide to put Grandpa in the hayfield today, even if he has died from natural causes. A pity, really. It would be rather nice to be able to choose a favourite beauty spot as one's last resting place! As for the rest of the story; certainly switching babies was a very wrong thing to do, but again, I don't know what the penalty might have been for that in Victorian times — or, for that matter, if something similar was done today!'

'Probably a hanging offence back then,' Maudie said. 'Anyway, the curator says you're welcome to go and read Miss Sanders' account for yourself if you wish.'

'I think I will. After all, I was the first one on the scene when Bull made his find. I'd like to be able to draw a line under the whole business.'

★   ★   ★

Once she had persuaded the curator to let her stay until she had read Eleanor Sanders' story, Maudie had turned back to see what she had written.

'My grandmother Polly Sanders, born Neville, came into this world shortly after Admiral Nelson's great victory at Trafalgar. Her father was a farm labourer on Lord Helmes' estate and she was brought up in a small cottage there. When she reached the age of twelve she went into service in the big house, first as a between-stairs maid, commonly called a tweeny, eventually rising to become a house parlourmaid. That was where she first met Sarah Stokes. Sally, they called her, and what a handsome young woman she was. In later years Granny told me that she had hair as black as jet, huge brown eyes and a delicate complexion.

'Sally had great plans for her life. Her ambition was to find a gentleman who would be willing to keep her in luxury. Life in a labouring man's cottage was not for her. Granny was shocked to hear her talk in that wanton way, yet she was fascinated by her too.

'Well, it happened! Sally came to Lord Roderick's attention. He was forty-five years of age by then, and still very handsome. He singled her out and very soon Sally was besotted by him. He promised her the moon. He had a wife living, a kindly woman who had given him five daughters, so marriage was out of the question, but Sally believed that he

248

would keep his promise to set her up in an establishment of her own and she would spend her life in luxury.

'In the year 1830 his wife gave birth to the longed-for heir to the title, and they named him Quentin. Sally's son Albert was born just three days later. That was when Sally was turned out of the house. Granny was never sure whether Lord Helmes gave her any money, but he certainly didn't live up to his promise to set her up as a lady. She was forced to return to her parents' home in disgrace, and lucky to be there, too, for they might well have turned her away. As it was, the vicar refused to baptize young Albie because he was born out of wedlock.

'That might have been the end of the story, except that when he was four months old Quentin Helmes died suddenly. His nursemaid found him in his cot one morning, quite dead. He had been well enough the night before when he'd been put to bed, but now he was gone and his nanny didn't dare to confess to it. It wasn't just a question of losing her job. Oh, no, it was far worse than that! She was afraid they'd accuse her of giving the child laudanum to stop him crying, which she hadn't done, and then they would hang her. As everyone knows, laudanum is a tincture of opium and it is often given to babies to keep them quiet, especially to unfortunate infants in those baby farms run by evil women.

'Granny had an idea that could save them all. She ran to Sally as fast as she could, and together they smuggled Albie into the house and up to the nurseries, where they dressed him in little Quentin's clothes. Together they buried the dead baby in a corner of a field that was lying fallow at Millwood farm. They believed that the vicar — if it should come to his ears that it was Albie who had died — would not permit an unbaptized child to be buried in holy ground. Sally left Llandyfan that same day, never to return. It was assumed by some that she had taken her child with her, while somehow the rumour persisted that he had died.

'Albert Stokes therefore was brought up as the son and heir of Lord Helmes and the deception was never discovered.

'Insofar as I know it, this is a true story. Written and signed by Eleanor Sanders, Llandyfan, September 1897.'

★ ★ ★

Maudie later went to share this story with the vicar's wife. After all, she had tried to help her connect the story to the Green family, and she deserved to know the outcome.

'In other words, it was nothing to do with them at all,' Mrs Blunt said.

'Not really, except that it was a still a local legend when Fanny Green was a girl. Her own grandmother must have been a contemporary of Polly and Sally, and of course everyone knew that the girl had a baby out of wedlock. They probably knew about her dalliance with Lord Helmes as well, even if they didn't know about the deception.'

'I suppose it was poetic justice in a way, Nurse. If this fantastic tale is to be believed, Roderick Helmes behaved badly towards Sally, not to mention his own wife, something which seems to have

251

happened all too frequently among the aristocracy in Queen Victoria's day. Although it could be that you and I are just as credulous as young Polly Neville was, believing everything she was told! Sally could well have been a scheming miss who used her looks to cheat an older man into giving her the lifestyle she wanted.'

'It wouldn't be the first time in the history of the world.'

'Mind you,' Mrs Blunt went on, trying to be fair, 'if Albie really was his son, and not the offspring of some village swain, it seems only right that the boy should have been brought up in luxury instead of possibly ending up in the workhouse, which was the fate of many in his position. Even though it was unintentional, it was fitting that he should succeed to the title in the end.'

'That's the thing, though, he didn't. He went to fight in the Crimea and died there. His father outlived him and the title died out.'

Mrs Blunt sighed at the unfairness of life. 'I do wonder what happened to Sally, don't you? Do you think her conscience ever troubled her? Did she marry and have other children? Did she somehow manage to keep track of Albie, or was she content to think of him living the life of luxury that she had once hoped for herself?'

'Oh, no you don't!' Maudie said. 'That's one mystery I certainly don't intend to follow up!

★   ★   ★

'I'm glad you aren't a member of the Mothers' Union,' Dick said drowsily, when they were lying side by side in their double bed that night.

'What on earth are you talking about?'

'They are still arguing about the inscription they want to put on that baby's headstone. When this story of yours gets out, how will they ever decide? He was originally buried as Albert Stokes, illegitimate son of a farm labourer, but in reality he was Quentin Helmes, a member of the aristocracy. It will call for the judgment of Solomon to sort that one out.'

'Quentin Helmes died in the Crimea. It says so on a memorial tablet inside the church.'

'You mean Albert Stokes did.'

Maudie raised herself on her elbow and pounded Dick with a pillow. 'Go to sleep!' she bawled. 'I've solved your wretched mystery for you! It doesn't matter to me what they put on his headstone. They can call him Old King Cole for all I care.'

'Maudie Bryant, you're beautiful when you're angry!' he told her. He reached out and turned off the bedside lamp.

27

Maudie agreed to let two couples tour the cottage on Saturday morning. There was really no point in putting it off any longer. Dick had the assurance of his bank manager that he could take out a mortgage, within limits, but there was no guarantee that their offer would be accepted by the parish council. Their home would go to the highest bidder.

The first arrivals were a very pleasant married couple from Midvale who wanted to downsize. The large brick house in which they had raised their family had been purchased by a builder who planned to turn it into three flats.

'Do you know if he means to rent them out, or will they be up for sale?' Dick asked. 'I'm based in Midvale and my wife and I are looking for something ourselves.'

'I'm sorry to dash your hopes, mate,' the man said, 'but our chap's got a waiting list a yard long. If I were you, I'd hang on here.'

'Can't be done, I'm afraid,' Dick told him sadly. 'Now, if you'd like to follow me, I'll show you upstairs.' Neither he nor Maudie felt up to extolling the amenities of the place, but they listened glumly while the husband spelled them out for his wife.

'It's handy for everything we need, Mabel. The church and the shop-cum-post-office are within walking distance, and there's a bus stop not far away in case we ever decide to give up driving. And there's a telephone already laid on. What do you think of the house itself?'

'It's very nice,' his wife said. 'I think we could be quite cosy here. We'd have to get rid of some of our furniture, of course, but we already knew that, didn't we? And there's the garden for you, dear; enough ground to keep you pottering about happily, but not so much that it would get the better of you!'

Maudie could bear it no longer. 'Are you interested in buying it, then?' she asked, crossing her fingers inside the pocket of her tweed skirt.

The man scratched his forehead. 'It has much to recommend it, but I'm afraid the price is too steep. I'll talk to the agent and see if the owners are prepared to come down a bit; but meanwhile, we'll have to go on looking. Thank you for showing us round. Come along, Mabel.'

Mabel smiled. 'Thank you so much! It's quite possible that we'll be back. I do hope we'll see you again. Goodbye!'

'Goodbye,' Maudie and Dick said in unison. They looked at each other, hardly daring to breathe. 'If they can beat the council down, there might be a chance for us!' Dick said. 'Perhaps there won't be any takers at this price; I always did say that three thousand quid is too steep.'

The second pair put Maudie's back up from the moment they entered the door. The man communicated in a series of grunts; he didn't need to say much when it was obvious that his wife was quite capable of doing all the talking!

'It's a bit pokey,' she complained, looking around Maudie's comfortable sitting room with distaste. 'Still, I suppose we could make something of it. We could throw out a bay window there and possibly build an extension onto the kitchen. And those beams will have to go. So twee! And I do hope you have indoor plumbing? Some of these old places are just too primitive.'

'Would you like to see upstairs?' Dick asked. 'There is quite a nice bathroom, actually and two very nice bedrooms.' Maudie gave him a furious look, not understanding that he felt he must come to the defence of the cottage when it seemed to be under attack, as if it was a stray cat that needed protection from fierce dogs.

'Do the curtains and carpets come with the house?' The woman frowned at Maudie. 'I can't say I think much of that home-spun weave; I prefer a nice floral chintz myself, but beggars can't be choosers.'

'Beggars?' Maudie's voice dripped frost.

'Oh, you know what I mean, dear! Since the war, it's been impossible to get nice things, and at least this stuff fits the windows.'

'They should do. I slaved for hours over them.'

'Oh, did you make them yourself?' She picked up the hem of one of the curtains, rubbing the fabric between her thumb and finger. Maudie bit back the urge to say something very rude indeed.

'And what about that carpet downstairs? It's a bit worn in places, but I suppose we'll have to make do until we can find something better.'

'I'm afraid we'll be taking the curtains and carpets with us,' Dick said, quite aware that the curtains might not fit the windows in their new home, wherever that might be, but sensing the need to defuse the situation before his wife's temper erupted.

'It's customary for fixtures and fittings to come with the house,' Mr Strong and Silent observed, speaking for the first time.

'Oh, they belong to me,' Maudie told him, through gritted teeth. 'I shall be taking them with me when we go. We intend to leave the lavatory and the kitchen sink, though.'

'I don't know what you mean, Mrs

er . . . ' He stared at her as though she was a creature from outer space.

'It doesn't matter,' his wife announced. 'We shan't be putting in an offer. This place isn't at all what we've been used to.'

Various retorts came to Maudie's mind — such as 'What have you been used to, then; Buckingham Palace?' — but with a great effort she managed to keep quiet. She saw the couple out, voicing insincere hopes that they would soon find something to suit them.

'Phew, what a pair!' Dick said, when Maudie had closed the front door with a little more force than was necessary. 'Of course, it's a common tactic, running a place down before trying to get a reduction in the price, but we'll have to make it clear that this sale has nothing to do with us. Never mind; it's all over for now. Shall I put the kettle on?'

But before they could receive the blessing of a nice hot cup of tea, the doorbell rang. 'What now?' Maudie hissed. 'Shall we keep quiet and pretend we're not at home?'

'Better go and answer it, love. It could

be Mrs Charming back again for another look at the worn patches in the Axminster.'

An apologetic couple waited on the doorstep, accompanied by a moody-looking teenage girl.

'I'm afraid we don't have an appointment to view, but if we could just have a quick look around?'

'Why not?' Maudie muttered, standing aside to let the trio in. If she refused they'd only come back another day, so she might as well get this over with.

The girl sat down in the kitchen while Dick accompanied her parents upstairs. She looked at Maudie accusingly. 'Is there anything to do in this place, Miss?'

'Inside the house, do you mean?'

'Naw! In this village.'

'Well, we have the Girl Guides, of course . . .

'Naw! Dances and that, and the flicks!'

'I'm afraid we have to go into Midvale for things like that. Llandyfan is not exactly the entertainment capital of Britain, but then we have other amusements to keep us busy.'

'Such as?'

'There are some lovely country walks round about, and some people enjoy birdwatching. We have the Women's Institute and the Mothers' Union . . . and nothing much that would interest you, my dear,' she finished lamely.

'If Mum and Dad try to make me live here, they've got another think coming!' The girl stood up as her parents entered the kitchen, with Dick bringing up the rear.

'Mum, Dad! This place stinks! Let's go!' She stalked towards the door, not looking back to see if her parents were coming. The mother looked at Maudie apologetically. 'I'm so sorry! Debbie is at that awkward age, you see. Come along, Frank!'

'It's quite all right,' Maude muttered. 'In fact, I'm delighted with the child!'

★ ★ ★

Maudie and Dick finally sat down to their cup of tea. 'Ouch!' she moaned. 'I don't think I can take much more of this! I feel quite bruised and battered after today's little encounters.'

'It's that last lot I feel sorry for,' Dick said. 'When we were upstairs the mother let slip that they want to move to a quiet country place because their Debbie is turning out to be a handful. You know the sort of thing: running with a tough crowd, staying out late at night, and the rest. They want the girl where they can keep an eye on her.'

'I doubt if bringing her to Llandyfan is the answer if she really is out of control. Easy enough for the girl to hitch-hike her way into Midvale or beyond if she hankers after the bright lights. You should have seen her face when I mentioned the Guides!'

'Luckily, young Debbie is not our problem. But listen, love, if you find this house-showing lark too stressful, I'll have a word with the agent. Let them send one of their people to squire prospective buyers around the house.'

'I suppose so.'

'Is there any more tea in that pot? I'm so parched I could drink the water out of the goldfish bowl.'

'We don't have a goldfish bowl.'

'No, but if we did, I could drain it.'

'Then the fish would die.'

'And we can't have that, so let's have another brew, love, okay?'

As Maudie got up to boil more hot water the telephone rang. 'Let it ring!' she said firmly. 'I am not going to answer that! If it's somebody else wanting to see the house without making a proper appointment, I'm not giving in to them. We are closed for the day!'

'We have to answer it, love,' Dick said, getting to his feet reluctantly. 'It could be an emergency call for me, or for you, come to that. If it is somebody wanting to see the house, I'll fob them off somehow.'

Maudie made fresh tea, recklessly throwing an extra spoonful into the pot. The resulting brew would be stronger than they usually liked it, but she felt she needed the reinforcement. And by the weary look on Dick's face, it appeared that he could use a bit of extra support as well.

'That was Cora Beasley.' Dick sat down

at the kitchen table, reaching for his cup.

'Oh, yes? Is she on the phone now?'

'No, she's gone. She just wanted me to give you a message. She said to tell you that she's been going through the estate papers, and she's found something she's sure you'll be interested in. Can you call in as soon as possible, she says.'

Maudie really didn't want to go. The mystery of the Helmes-Stokes baby was solved now, or at least they had learned as much as they were ever likely to discover about that business. She had no illusions that another memoir had turned up that would shed more light on the affair. Mrs Beasley was probably all excited over some official papers showing the transaction between her father-in-law and the widowed Lady Victoria when the estate was sold.

Still, she probably had nobody else who would show the slightest interest in what, to her, would be a fascinating glimpse into her own family's past. And Cora Beasley had shown great kindness in offering Maudie and Dick a place to stay. Surely it wasn't asking too much for

Maudie to give up an hour or two of her own fulfilling life to cheer up a lonely person?

'I'll pop over first thing on Monday morning,' she said.

'You do that, love,' Dick said. 'And I'll go and see the house agent and make it quite clear to him that we won't put up with any more nonsense. You've been looking rather tired lately, old girl, and I won't have you put upon.'

266

28

Monday morning found Maudie languishing in bed. 'Do you think you could make your own breakfast this morning?' she asked, when Dick emerged from the bathroom with a shining morning face. 'I don't feel quite the thing.'

'You're not coming down with something, are you, love? Should I give Dr Dean a ring and ask him to make a house call?'

'Don't be silly. I'll be all right. I could do with another half-hour, that's all.'

'Would you like me to bring you up something on a tray?'

'Just a cup of tea, please. I don't feel like eating yet.'

Later, when Dick had called up the stairs to say goodbye, she listened for the sound of the car being driven off, and then she rolled over onto her side. She would just doze for a few minutes and then she would make an effort. There

267

were no patients to attend to today, but she would cycle over to see Mrs Beasley and get that crossed off her to-do list. On the way she would call in at the surgery, now being held in the converted gate-house of the estate, and see how Nurse Gregg was getting on.

After their recent chat, she felt it important to make sure that everything was going smoothly there, and hoped that her visit would be construed as sympathetic interest rather than meddling.

It was with great dismay that she awoke later to find that she had slept the morning away. Peering fuzzily at the alarm clock on the bedside table, she saw that it was almost lunchtime. Nurse Gregg would have said goodbye to the final patient of the morning by now; and as for Cora Beasley, what on earth would she be thinking? Maudie would have to phone to apologize.

'That's quite all right, Nurse,' Mrs Beasley said when she did so. 'I'm sure you must be worn out with all you've had to do lately. I expect you needed the extra rest. As for me, I hadn't planned to do anything else this morning and I was able to use the time sorting out a great pile of snaps that have accumulated in my desk. I meant to put them into albums, but I ended up throwing a lot of them in the dustbin. You know the sort of thing I mean: people cut off at the knees, or looking as if they've had a sudden shock!'

'I see.'

'So do come this afternoon. I can't wait to show you what I've found!'

★   ★   ★

After a quick bath, followed by a scrappy lunch of bread and cheese and a rather wizened apple, Maudie set off, hoping that the cycle ride in a brisk wind would brighten her up. But by the time she arrived at the manor house, she still felt as if she was wading through treacle.

Pull yourself together, Maudie Bryant! she admonished herself. Stop acting like a dying duck and try to look interested. Hear what Mrs Beasley has to say, sip your cup of tea if she offers you one, and then go on your way, duty done!

It was hard to remain dull in the face of Mrs Beasley's cheerful mood. Maudie followed the lady into the study, where the boxes from the bank were stacked up in one corner.

'Here you are, then, Nurse! This is what I found!'

Maudie accepted the document, frowning at the copperplate writing. The legal jargon made it hard for her to understand what it was all about, but at last she gathered that it had to do with the transfer of a number of cottages from the estate to the parish council.

'What exactly am I looking for here?' she asked, looking up at Mrs Beasley in some bewilderment.

'The cooper's house and two adjoining properties on Church Road.'

'Yes?'

'For goodness' sake, Nurse! It's your cottage, isn't it?'

'Oh, I see.' Maudie tried to read on, but none of it made any sense to her.

'Oh, give it to me!' Mrs Beasley snapped, snatching the papers back. She reminded Maudie of a teacher she'd had at school, where you got a rap across the knuckles if you didn't answer quickly enough in the hated mental arithmetic lessons.

'This document was drawn up in 1897,' she began. 'That was when Queen Victoria celebrated her diamond jubilee. In celebration of that event, my late father-in-law deeded the cottages to the parish council on a sort of permanent loan. I seem to recall that the idea was to use them as almshouses for deserving old people of the parish, which of course would have been a wonderful alternative to the workhouse!

'If you had turned over the page, you would have seen a clause giving a member of the Beasley family the right of veto if the cottages should ever be sold. Two of those cottages were sold before the war, and only your home remains in the hands of parish council.'

'And it is up for sale now,' Maudie said sadly, wondering why Mrs Beasley was bothering her with all this. It might be of historical interest, but why rub her nose in it?

'Yes, Nurse! We know that, don't we! But what is my name?'

'Your name?' Maudie asked stupidly. 'Er, Cora Beasley, I suppose.'

'Exactly. And what does that mean? Why, that I have the right of veto when the last remaining cottage is to be sold. I've given this a lot of thought, Nurse, and I've come to a decision. Either the cottage will be offered to you, to purchase at fair market value, or a rental agreement will be set up for you. Either way, you will not have to leave your home!'

★   ★   ★

'Oh what a beautiful morning, oh what a beautiful day!' Maudie belted out the words from the musical *Oklahoma* as she freewheeled down the lanes on her way home, alarming a shire horse in a nearby field and sending it galloping off. All her tiredness had disappeared as if it had never been. Taking her feet off the pedals, she swung her legs in the air, like a child released from school. They were saved! Oh, joy!

On arriving home, she wrenched the hated 'For Sale' sign from its place on the lawn, threw it to the ground and jumped on it.

'What did you want to go and do that for?'

Startled, she stared at the speaker, a haughty-looking woman who had come around the side of the house unnoticed. She hoped she'd remembered to lock the back door before she left; in her state of mind there was no telling what she'd done.

'I was speaking to you!'

'Can I help you?' Maudie asked, with a delicious sense of what was coming next.

'I came to view these premises, but there doesn't seem to be anyone in. Are you the cleaning woman? Do you have a key?'

Maudie was aware of her dishevelled appearance, but she couldn't care less. 'Did you make an appointment?'

The woman looked her up and down. 'Is that necessary?'

'No,' Maudie said, with a smile that would have done credit to a crocodile about to swallow his prey in one gulp. 'Not necessary at all. This house is no longer for sale.'

'I say, this is a bit much! A moment ago that sign was there for all to see! I shall complain to the estate agents about this! If this isn't false advertising, I don't know what is.'

'As you can see, I have removed the sign,' Maudie said. 'Good day to you, Madam!' Having wheeled her bicycle round to the back of the house, she fumbled for her key and let herself into the house. *Her* house.

★ ★ ★

That evening, Maudie and Dick celebrated by going to the Royal Oak for drinks. 'Fair market value,' Dick mused, as he sipped his half-pint. 'I wonder what that means? The three thousand they were asking in the beginning, or the twelve hundred Sam suggested?'

'Mrs Beasley thought they'd look for three independent appraisals and go from there. It might result in something affordable.'

'So what should we do? It might be better to rent if they give us that option.'

Maudie shook her head. 'When you pay rent you never see that money again. I think that if we managed to own the place we'd have something to show for it in the end.'

They sat in silence for a while until Dick suddenly thumped the table, making Maudie jump. 'I've thought of a way we can have the best of both worlds, if only they'd go for it!'

'Yes?'

'We pay rent, with an option to buy.'

'That sounds reasonable.'

'But listen to this, old girl. If we decide to buy, the amount of rent we've paid up to then is deducted from the price!'

'You'll be lucky!'

'But why not? It might work if we negotiate it in the beginning.'

'It's worth a try!' Maudie said. 'Let's go

home, Dick. Shall we have an early night?'

Saluting the landlord, they walked out into the gathering gloom and set out for home.

29

'Ow! I think I've got what you had,' Dick moaned, clutching his stomach. He had crawled out of bed at five o'clock in the morning, making a dash for the bathroom. Now he was back in the bedroom, hunched over on the side of the bed, looking green about the gills.

'You can't have caught anything from me,' Maudie told him. 'You don't have the same symptoms at all. Just get back under the covers while I fetch the thermometer.'

Five minute later she announced that his temperature was normal, but his tongue looked horrible. 'Did you have anything unusual to eat yesterday?'

He paused as another round of cramps came and went. 'Only those tomato sandwiches you packed for me.'

'Dick?'

'Oh, all right! If you must know I did feel in need of a little something when we were out on a case. We stopped at a mobile canteen for a cup of tea by the roadside.'

'And what else?'

Dick blushed. 'Just a sausage roll. Well, two or three sausage rolls, actually.'

'I suspect the meat must have been off. And if you will insist on packing in more calories than you need to keep going, you deserve to get sick. I suppose there's one good thing about getting the colly-wobbles, you may lose a bit of weight in a hurry.'

'A man expects to get a little sympathy from his wife when he's at death's door!' Dick moaned.

'Yes, well, it's obvious that you can't go to work in this state. I'll call in your apologies and then I'll mix up a dose of something for you. Something nasty-tasting that will do you good.'

Dick groaned and pulled the pillow over his face.

At a reasonable hour, Maudie contacted the police station at Midvale, identifying herself as Nurse Bryant to give weight to her diagnosis of Dick's ailment.

A cheerful woman who Maudie assumed to be a female police officer promised to pass the message on, although by coincidence Inspector Goodwood, Dick's boss, was also under the weather and he wouldn't be in either.

'I imagine they've both caught the same bug, Mrs Bryant.'

'Yes. The sausage roll and fall-off-your-diet bug,' Maudie told her.

'I beg your pardon?'

'Never mind. I expect they'll live to tell the tale. Good morning!'

Now what? Maudie wondered. She'd better not go out, in case Dick was really ill and she had to send for Dr Dean. Vacuuming would disturb him. There was a pound of stewing beef in the larder that she'd meant to put into an oven casserole that day, with onions and turnip and carrots, but the smell of food cooking might make him feel worse. She knew how that could happen. Yesterday, she had popped into the Copper Kettle to buy a jam doughnut, when the aroma of coffee had hit her senses like a wave of ozone at the seaside and she'd had to leave in a hurry.

She stood still in the middle of the sitting room, her eyes wide. Could it be? Could it possibly be? *Maudie Bryant, how could you be so stupid? And you call yourself a midwife!*

Hardly daring to believe it, she thought about the signs and symptoms. All that tiredness. The sudden craving for jam doughnuts. The sudden distaste for lovely fresh-brewed coffee. What she had taken to be the onset of the menopause was in fact the early stages of pregnancy! It was true that she'd lost a bit of weight recently — in fact, she'd gloated over it when Dick had bemoaned his own increasing girth — but that, too, often happened early on. And there were other signs that she'd ignored because she'd been so involved in her work and the worry about the cottage.

Maudie Bryant, aged forty-one and fast approaching forty-two, was about to have her first child! She felt herself almost overwhelmed by the joy that surged through her. She mustn't bank on it yet, she reminded herself. It all had to be confirmed before she could think about knitting little pink or blue bootees. Neither would she let Dick into the secret yet awhile. It would be too cruel to get his hopes up, only to see them dashed later.

All day long she hugged the precious secret to herself. She knew there could be risks involved. She was getting on a bit for a first pregnancy, and if she miscarried before it came to term, she might not be given a second chance.

Although she was healthy, she had less energy than the young mothers in her care, many of whom were half her age. Getting up in the middle of the night to feed a demanding baby would be taxing. On the other hand, she and Dick would surely have more patience than younger parents when it came to dealing with the Terrible Twos or the teenage tantrums.

Teenagers! Now there was a thought! By the time their son or daughter was launched on the world, Dick would be a pensioner, with Maudie not far behind. She thought of the sullen girl who had sneered at Llandyfan when her parents had come to view the cottage. Baby

Bryant would never behave like that! He or she would attend the dear little village school, join the Cubs or the Brownies, attend worship in St John's church. Best of all, the child would grow up in a peaceful world, knowing nothing of the two world wars that Maudie and Dick had seen.

She heard the toilet flush. Poor Dick was up again, and she had forgotten all about the dose she'd threatened him with. She decided to take him a cup of tea instead. It might settle his stomach.

★ ★ ★

The time had come. Dr Dean had confirmed that Maudie was 'with child' as he put it.

'That sounds very Biblical,' she remarked.

He raised his eyebrows. 'What would you like me to say? I can't very well tell you you're 'in kitten', can I?'

Maudie was flabbergasted. 'It's not like you to be jocular, Dr Dean. Anybody would think you've had good news too.'

282

'I have!' he said, his usually stern expression softening. 'I'm engaged to be married!'

'Oh, how lovely! Congratulations! Is it Valerie?'

'Valerie? How on earth did you hear about her? No, it's Susan, my receptionist here.'

For one wild moment, Maudie thought he was talking about Miss Holmes, the dragon who for many years had guarded Dr Malory's surgery from all comers, remembering in time that she had retired and been replaced by a jolly young woman with red hair.

'I hope you'll be very happy, Doctor,' she said, meaning it sincerely. Dr Dean had often been a thorn in her side, but in her newfound happiness she wanted everyone to share the joy.

* * *

'I want to tell you about a woman I know,' she told Dick that evening, when they were sitting at the fireside with cups of cocoa.

'Who is that, then?'

'She's a maternity patient, actually.'

'One of yours, I suppose.'

'In a way. Well, Dick, she's over forty, and she's just found out that she's going to have her first baby. What do you think of that?'

For a moment, a wistful expression appeared on Dick's face, and she hugged herself at the thought of what was to come.

'I take it she's pleased about it?' he enquired.

'Ecstatic! The thing is, she hasn't told her husband yet, and she's not sure what his reaction is going to be.'

'Have they been married long?'

'Just a few months. In fact, they were married in St John's church on the third Saturday in July.'

She waited until the penny dropped. Dick's jaw dropped open.

'Maudie! What are you trying to tell me? You wouldn't pull an old man's leg, would you? You don't mean . . . oh, my gosh, Maudie! Come here, you wonderful, gorgeous woman, you!'

He pulled her to her feet and they stood swaying on the middle of the living-room rug, hugging and kissing, with tears rolling down their cheeks.

'I'm going to be a dad!' he cried, sniffing. 'Oh, Maudie, you've made me so happy! I'm going to be the best father any boy has ever had! I can promise you that!'

'Or girl,' she reminded him. 'The baby could be a girl, you know!'

'Of course, it was just a figure of speech. Just wait till I tell the chaps at work!'

'Oh, you mustn't tell anybody yet,' Maudie said. 'You mustn't say a thing until the first three months are safely past.'

'Oh, that's just an old wives' tale, surely?'

'Never mind about that, Dick Bryant. This old wife insists!'

30

Another Christmas was coming. This would be the first Christmas they were spending under the same roof together, although Dick had spent the day here during the previous two festive seasons.

'We won't be able to use these glass baubles next year,' Maudie pointed out as they decorated their little fir tree together. 'The baby will be crawling by then, and trying to reach up to grab them. In fact, having a tree at all may not be such a good idea, unless we have a miniature one to stand on a table.'

'We'll have to supply the little one with plenty of safe toys to keep it busy, then.' Dick had already made a set of building bricks which he intended to paint in bright colours.

'We can't keep calling the baby 'it', as if it's a cat or a dog, and it's awkward saying 'he or she' all the time. Can't we think of a suitable nickname for Baby Bryant?'

'Rover,' suggested Dick. 'That's what I meant to call the dog I never did get.'

'Don't be so silly! Whoever heard of a baby called Rover?' Maudie said, laughing; but somehow the nickname stuck, and they found themselves referring to the child in that way from then on. They couldn't plan a getaway at Easter because Rover was likely to arrive then. The spare room would be turned into a nursery for Rover.

* * *

They had decided not to buy each other presents that Christmas, assuring each other than the coming baby was gift enough. Not only that, after a few happy hours wandering around the big department store in Midvale, they had realized that kitting out a new baby was a costly venture.

Dick wanted a Silver Cross pram for his child, the best that money could buy.

'Order one if you must, but it's not coming into this house before the baby arrives,' Maudie said firmly.

'Why ever not?'

'Just because.'

Dick frowned at her. 'You're not worried about that old superstition, surely? You're an educated woman, a midwife, for heaven's sake. You can take it from me, old girl, nothing is going to happen to this baby, even if we park the pram in the coal shed.'

'I know, but I don't care! I'm just not taking any chances.'

Dick rolled his eyes, but he let it go. His married colleagues had warned him about this kind of thing. His chief, Inspector Bob Goodwood, was the father of four practically grown-up children, and he had plenty of advice to hand out. 'Women tend to get funny ideas when they are expecting, Bryant, and if you know what's good for you you'll keep your thoughts to yourself. Besides, if, heaven forbid, something did go wrong, and you'd thrown your weight around over some of her idiotic notions, your wife would never let you forget it.'

Maudie couldn't object to having the nursery prepared in good time, though, so

Dick distempered the walls in a sort of rose-tinted cream and put up a frieze depicting Beatrix Potter characters. In time, they would collect all the books, and when Rover was of an age to be read to, he (or she) could lie in his cot and be able to identify the familiar pictures of Benjamin Bunny, Mrs Tiggywinkle and Pigling Bland.

Maudie had already begun sewing muslin draperies for the 'treasure cot' that would replace the initial Moses basket, and Dick was unwise enough to wonder aloud how it was unlucky to have a pram in the house but not the cradle. She was furious, grabbed the last slice of Battenberg cake that he had earmarked for himself, and told him that if he was hungry he could jolly well make do with bread and dripping.

'It's not like you to be spiteful,' he said plaintively. 'Can't a chap think aloud without getting his head bitten off?'

'I'm allowed to be spiteful, I'm pregnant!' she said, and burst out laughing. The pair of them sat there grinning like fools, delighting in the knowledge that they were soon to be parents.

* * *

As soon as their happy news was made public, word of Maudie's condition spread round the parish like greased lightning, as her old grandmother used to say.

'You're in for it now, Nurse,' the sexton said gloomily. 'All them broken nights and smelly nappies. Take it from me, you'll wish you'd stayed single.'

'Thank you, Mr Pratt, you could be right,' Maudie answered, too happy to be bothered by doom and gloom. 'At least I'll have somebody to take care of me in my old age.'

The vicar was delighted for them, although less than tactful in his reception of the news.

'This reminds me of Zechariah and Elizabeth in the Bible,' he remarked. 'Elizabeth was barren until she was 'well stricken in years', and then she produced a son, who became John the Baptist.'

'Harold, really!' Mrs Blunt reproved him.

'Why, what have I said? I was only pointing out how happy Mrs Bryant must be.'

Maudie laughed ruefully. 'When I heard that story in Sunday School, I somehow got hold of the idea that Elizabeth was a hundred years old; and believe me, that's how I feel some mornings when the alarm goes off.'

'I don't think the Bible actually spells out her age,' the vicar said, rubbing his chin. 'All we know is that she was well past the age for bearing children when the Angel Gabriel appeared to Zechariah and said . . .'

'Thank you, Harold,' Joan Blunt said. 'I think that Nurse has got the message.'

★   ★   ★

Mrs Hatch at the village shop was determined to have her say to add to Llandyfan's collective words of wisdom. As postmistress she felt she had that right.

'Why don't you open a post office savings account for the little one? If you buy a stamp each week it will add up in no time, and having a bit put by is always useful.'

'I think I will,' Maudie said.

'No time like the present, I always say. Do you have half a crown to spare to start it off?'

Maudie peered into her purse and managed to come up with the coin in question.

'Now then,' Mrs Hatch said briskly. 'Name?'

'Maudie Bryant, of course.' The older woman must be already showing signs of senility if she couldn't recall who Maudie was. Or was she simply being officious?

The postmistress tutted in exasperation. 'I meant the baby's name, dear.'

'Oh, right. Rover. Rover Bryant.'

31

'I wish I'd seen there to see the old girl's face when you told her we've decided to call the baby Rover!' Dick threw back his head and roared with laughter. 'Mind you, we should come to a decision soon. I've been giving it a lot of thought, and I vote for Barbara for a girl, or Steven for a boy.'

'You only like Barbara because you fancy Barbara Stanwyck,' Maudie complained. 'Perhaps you'd like me to call a boy after some Hollywood film star, too. How about Errol, or Tyrone?'

'You can forget about that!'

'I thought so! Mind you, Miss Stanwyck's real name was Ruby Rouse. I wouldn't mind Ruby, and you could still have Steven.'

'I think we'll stick with Rover,' said Dick. 'When we do get a dog, you can call him Errol if you like.'

★ ★ ★

Along with half the people of Llandyfan, Maudie and Dick stood in front of the parish hall with their hands linked, singing *Auld Lang Syne*. The church bells rang out loud and clear to welcome the New Year in. How good it was to hear those peals again! The ringing of church bells had been forbidden during the war, when their tolling had been reserved to spread the alarm from coast to coast in the event of the invasion taking place.

Maudie sighed happily. 1950 had seen some of the most remarkable events of her life. The world was at peace again. Her wedding had taken place in July. Then, after many weeks of worry, the question of where they would live had at last been settled.

'Come now, Mrs Bryant! Rover is a dog's name. You surely don't intend to lumber an innocent child with that? What would Vicar say when you brought the baby to the font?'

Maudie's cheeks turned crimson. 'Of course not. My husband wants to get a dog, you know, and that's what he means to call it. Rover, or possibly Champ. I'm afraid I spoke without thinking. I'm so tired these days I don't know what I'm saying, half the time.'

'You poor dear! Of course you're exhausted, having a baby at your age. No wonder you look so pale. You must let me make him a nice cup of tea, dear, with a drop of something in it.'

'I don't mind if I do, Mrs Hatch. Thank you very much! I'll have to say no to the drop of something, though. Doctor's orders!'

'Not even medicinal brandy?'

'Not even that.'

'Just a lot of killjoys, them doctors. Speaking of doctors, did you hear the latest about Dr Dean? He's going to marry that Melanie Gregg.'

'I'm afraid that's not true, Mrs Hatch, and I know that for a fact.'

'Aw! I did hope it would happen in Llandyfan so we could see them leaving the church as man and wife. I do love a nice wedding.'

'I believe it's true that Dr Dean is engaged, but Nurse Gregg is not his intended bride.' Maudie had a nasty idea that Dr Dean had shared his plans with her in confidence, but she mustn't let unfounded rumours persist. 'You go and put the kettle on, Mrs Hatch, and I'll tell you what I know when we're having our cup of tea.'

The crowning glory was yet to come. Her baby was due before she and Dick would celebrate the first anniversary of their wedding, and then they would be a real family. The lovely young Princess Elizabeth, who had welcomed her little daughter Princess Anne into the world just four months ago, had also given birth to her first child before her first wedding anniversary. That was little Charles, who would one day be king.

It was highly unlikely that Maudie would produce a second child, yet she was happier with her lot than she had ever dreamed it was possible to be. She didn't own palaces or diamonds, and her husband wasn't a fairytale prince like the Duke of Edinburgh, yet she would not change places with their future queen for all the world. She had her own dear little cottage and her very own prince charming in the shape of rugged, reliable Dick Bryant. She glanced up at her husband and smiled.

We do hope that you have enjoyed reading this large print book.

Did you know that all of our titles are available for purchase?

We publish a wide range of high quality large print books including:
Romances, Mysteries, Classics
General Fiction
Non Fiction and Westerns

Special interest titles available in large print are:
The Little Oxford Dictionary
Music Book, Song Book
Hymn Book, Service Book

Also available from us courtesy of Oxford University Press:
Young Readers' Dictionary
(large print edition)
Young Readers' Thesaurus
(large print edition)

For further information or a free brochure, please contact us at:
Ulverscroft Large Print Books Ltd.,
The Green, Bradgate Road, Anstey,
Leicester, LE7 7FU, England.
Tel: (00 44) **0116 236 4325**
Fax: (00 44) **0116 234 0205**